AUDRIC'S WAY

Ken Souyave

FIRST EDITION

ISBNs:
Paperback: 978-1-80227-414-1
eBook: 978-1-80227-415-8

Contents

Place Names

Londinium – the capital of Roman Britain and originally a settlement predating Roman rule on the current site of the City of London. It was significantly depopulated after the Romans left Britain and during the few centuries beyond.

Lundenwic – a relatively densely built-up settlement used by craftsmen and traders, only a short distance from Londinium.

Hexham, Northumbria – a church was erected on the site of the current Hexham Abbey after a grant of lands was made in the late seventh century to Abbot Wilfrid, then Bishop of Eoforwic. It was largely built of materials salvaged from nearby Roman ruins.

Ripon, Northumbria – A stone church was erected here during a similar period to the church in Hexham to replace a former timber-built monastery. This building was also under the control of Abbot Wilfrid.

Northumbria – a medieval kingdom contrived from two former territories, Deira and Bernicia. It stretched from the current Humber Estuary to well north of Lindisfarne and up to the Lothian border.

Eoforwic – (or Eboracum in Roman times) is the seventh-century name adopted at that time for what we now call York.

Elmet – a territory comprising parts of current West and South Yorkshire and North Derbyshire.

Mercia – a medieval kingdom covering a large area of central England south of the Humber Estuary.

Tadcaster – this name was not in use in the seventh century, but part of Audric's adventure took place in a village along the same route now travelled between Leeds and York.

Lindsey – a small, medieval kingdom south of the current Humber Estuary and bound to the south by the then Kingdom of Mercia.

Rochester and Canterbury, Kent – early cathedral towns with strong religious significance and centres for widespread trading.

Characters

I hope you will find all the characters real, but the following are known to have existed.

Abbot Wilfrid

Archbishop Theodore – Archbishop of Canterbury from 668-690

Wulfhere – King of Mercia from 658-675

AEthelred – succeeded his brother Wulfhere and was king until 704

Ecgfrith – King of Northumbria from 670-685

And here are important characters in Audric's progress through life:

Audric is a medieval name meaning 'wise ruler'

Aldren and Oldred – Overlords controlling major tribes in Northumbria under the rule of King Ecgfrith

Sher – An eagle that has an uncanny connection with Audric and Tork

Star – A dog that changes from vicious foe to lifelong friendly companion

Tork – A dwarf-like man who became Audric's lifelong friend

Morgan – A mystical elderly man who changes Audric's life from a young age

Part 1

From Child to Man

Chapter 1

My name is Tork. I'm not your typical human - dwarf in stature, but a giant in spirit. The main character in the story that unfolds is Audric; just fifteen years old when my master, Morgan, felt it was time for me to move on, and I joined Audric, forming a life-long friendship.

Whilst young, Audric seemed wise beyond his years. He had been born to parents who were settlement travellers moving around the countryside, mainly in the kingdom of Northumbria, working the land to earn their keep. Times proved difficult, following waves of invasions over many decades by European neighbours looking to prosper on new fertile lands or act as mercenaries for the overlords of existing kingdoms. Attacks on settlements were always a possibility as new arrivals looked to capture their own pieces of land.

One such raid sent the people of Audric's settlement scattering to different parts of the countryside, separating the eleven-year-old from his parents. Many settlers were slain, but he escaped with a small number of his fellow travellers. Despite a wide search, Audric never found his parents and feared they may have died in the attack. Whilst well cared for, it was a difficult life, always on the go, often in extreme conditions during the winter months. Audric soon learnt many skills essential to survival; hunting, scavenging, horse-riding and being at one with nature.

As time went on, he had an intense desire to see if he could find his parents, assuming they might have survived the raid.

Fit and strong, though still growing, it was time for Audric to go his own way. He did so with the blessing of his surrogate family, who had brought him up during these last four years. They knew many well-established travellers' routes and, over the years, they had made many enquiries to find his parents without success. Despite all of this, Audric's adventurous spirit was driving him to seek new opportunities and, with good fortune, maybe stumble on his parents one day.

Audric walked between settlements staying a few days here and a few days there. One day, he reached my master's home, deep in woodland north of Otterburn, in the heart of Northumbria. He had rarely stayed in or near such an unusual home and was being curious when he knocked on the door. My master was out collecting plants from the woods when we first met. I'm sure he was more surprised to see me than I was to observe him. I could see a strapping, well-built young man with long straggly black hair and good looks.

What Audric saw probably shocked him.

"By God!" he exclaimed. "I'm sorry to gawp. My name is Audric, and I was taken by the strange character of your dwelling as I walked through the woods. I was curious to see more, so felt compelled to knock."

I held my smile back and said with a degree of seriousness, "Aye, lad, have ya never seen a dwarf before? My name's Tork."

Audric held his tongue but continued to gaze intensely, observing my short stature, mass of dark red frizzy hair and flimsy clothing that exposed my muscular body and tanned complexion.

Audric finally responded. "Sorry, you took me aback; I've never seen anyone quite like you. Are you one of the invaders from across the sea?"

"Nah," was my reply, "just a quirk of birth, I think, but strangely I have no recollection of my parents. I seem to have been with my master forever, and he says he is not my father, though he has looked after me as if he were."

"Where is your master?" asked Audric. "Does he look like you?"

"You're a polite lad, Audric. Come on in and satisfy your curiosity. You can wait here if you like."

I watched him walk in, and he moved in a confident manner. Despite his ragged clothing, Audric had a real presence about him. I immediately thought that my master would enjoy his company, especially as he was ageing and in ill health. Anything that lifted his spirits might bring back the sparkle that used to be in his eyes. I reflected that it was many years since my master had used his mystical powers.

Audric was pacing slowly around the room, taking in the setting. Now, he seemed less curious about me and more interested in the array of glass bottles holding colourful solutions, plus the unusual display of copper pots and pans and green plants growing on the sills.

Audric asked, "What's in the bottles?"

"Best if Master answers that question, but I can get you a drink in the meantime."

"Just what I need," replied Audric as he sat on a nearby stool, still taking in the strange surroundings when the door opened slowly, and the face of an elderly man poked in.

Before Audric or I could say anything, my master quietly mumbled, "You are not what I expected, very young; very young indeed. My name is Morgan. Welcome to our home."

We both looked at Morgan quizzically, wondering what he meant by 'expected.' I knew Master would explain all in good time, and Audric seemed unconcerned, slightly in awe of what he could see. Master had that way about him, when needed, despite his current frailty. His eyes were already warming to the task, whatever that was to be, and Audric seemed to be entranced.

Looking and assessing Morgan, Audric noted the unusual outer coat, a mix of animal hides with shades of brown, black and white, cut to finery he'd rarely seen. A plain leather cap covered his grey and white hair, and a rueful smile came to his face, making him appear years younger. Morgan was old and moved slowly, but he was still the one holding the stage.

Master broke the silence, "Please eat with us, the food is already prepared, and you are welcome to stay overnight."

Audric didn't need to be asked twice after days with next to no food. I set the table, and we sat around eating and drinking Master's wine with little but polite conversation, though I could tell Master had a plan for this young man.

"Enough for tonight," said Morgan as he got to his feet; then, we all headed for our bunks. I tried to daydream about what Master had in mind, but I fell asleep, too tired to think.

When I woke, Master and Audric were already in deep conversation. I was about to back away when Master called me over.

"Join us, Tork, there are no secrets between you and I after all these years, and this does involve your future."

It would seem his plan was in play, and I might have no say in the matter.

Morgan drew us both in with a show of hands, and we huddled around the burning embers of the fire.

"Tork," said Master with a deep voice. At that point, I knew things were going to change forever.

"You know that I'm of an age well beyond the dreams of many people, and my body is frail. I am now ready to retreat to a place where my physical body is no longer needed, but my mind can take stock of the past. In this place, whilst I will have wonderful memories, I will be entirely alone until my spirit dies and I no longer exist." Master looked at both of us. "I hope you and Audric can become life-long friends as I believe you have a mission together. Tork knows that I possess certain mystical powers that have been passed down through generations. Their aim is to prevent evil in the world and ensure we are ruled in a way that is most beneficial to society as a whole. With my time coming to an end, it was inherent in me to put out ethereal thoughts to attract the mind of someone like Audric who has a desire to follow a similar path that I and other generations have pursued."

Master gazed at Audric with his piercing blue eyes. "Audric, I can see that you are amazed to have been chosen. I know you are destined for a world very different to your current way of life."

Morgan then turned to me, "You will need to work together with great respect. Audric is not me and will be his own man, just as you are your own man. You don't need to refer to him as Master, but working together, I promise you will achieve more than apart."

I edged back from our huddle and felt full of many questions and concerns, but suddenly, my mind settled, and the way ahead seemed clear. I was content, even happy, about the future. "Master, when will this happen, and what about Sher?" I asked.

"Dear Tork, you have been a wonderful companion and helped save my life several times, but I am ready to rest. I have talked with you about this in recent times as my mind and body have declined, so I hope you are well prepared for my demise. I can no longer drift from day to day. You and Audric will leave here tomorrow, and I will go to the haven of my choice before the sun goes down. As for Sher, he will be with you when needed, as always. I have explained to Audric how Sher must go his own way but can be relied upon when the time is right. Come to the doorway."

We walked out and looked up to the clear blue sky.

"Audric, put your arm out," instructed Morgan. "Come, Sher."

The words reverberated through the woodland. Seconds passed, and we all waited with anticipation. A dark image appeared in the distant sky, growing slowly bigger. Now the outline of a bird was evident. Then the wide wingspan of a large eagle showed clearly, helping it to glide in gracefully and land on the extended arm.

"Wow, he's magnificent," said Audric, who had been entirely silent whilst Master was talking.

I looked at Sher and Audric in complete harmony and then turned to observe my master. The glaze in his eyes suggested both excitement and a degree of sadness. At that point, I knew Audric, Sher and I were the future.

Chapter 2

By midday, we were on our way and, without discussion, instinctively set off in a southerly direction, aiming to pick up a trail down to the lowlands of Northumbria. Master had made it clear that we were to move on whilst he would remain at home on his own and, in time, he would pass on his powers to Audric. Sadness came over me, and Audric could see this.

"Cheer up," he said. "We have a great adventure ahead. I don't think either of us are permanent settlers, and we can explore the nation and maybe travel overseas if the opportunity arises. We will make our fortune; if not in coinage, then we shall be rich in knowledge."

I smiled as already he reminded me of my master, and then I thought how strange not to call Audric Master. "Well, lead the way, my bonny lad, for every step is a step nearer that fortune," I responded.

We strode on and talked about the practicalities of our journey, such as which was the best settlement to head for and how we might pick up work or earn our keep. We were both experienced at looking after ourselves in the countryside, but a roof over our heads was always appreciated, particularly in the winter months. This would mean living and working in fresh communities and meeting new people. Sometimes the protection offered by large groups of people might save our lives, as my master and I had occasionally found out.

"We'll head for Hexham, Tork," Audric suggested with a calm and determined voice. "I've passed through a few good settlements down that way and may be able to find some people I've met before."

After a long stint in the saddle, we picked out a small glade near the riverbank as the sun went down over the steep surrounding hills. Whilst it was warm, rain began to fall heavily, so we created a shelter using offcuts from the trees, bracken and the leather hides we carried. There was one flagon of wine and only food for a couple of days. We would be hunting again soon. I'd seen a few rabbits and a pack of wild boars nearby, but we were ready for an easy evening after a long walk. In time, we would need horses to speed up our travels, but our resources were limited for now.

After sharing the wine, it was easy to settle down for a good night's sleep, though the rain continued to rattle down and lightning lit up the night sky over the hills. Audric seemed to fall asleep as soon as his head hit the floor, but I lay listening to the passage of the river and pondering our future.

It seemed like hours that I tried to get off to sleep, but there was no let-up in the rain. Suddenly there was a roaring sound, and fear gripped my throat. I rolled out of the shelter at speed, looked up the valley and saw with horror a torrent of water coming towards us.

"Flash flood! Get out now!" I yelled, knowing it was probably already too late.

I grabbed Audric by his collar, but the wall of water hit us before we had a chance to get out of the shelter. For a few seconds, it was as though we had been launched to sea in a makeshift boat, but it soon fell apart and sent us spinning and turning, gasping for breath as the water sucked us down. The power of the water was overwhelming, but the cold revived our senses as we fought to save our lives. At one point, I was thrown high on the crest of a wave and caught sight of Audric, following me, clinging desperately to a small branch, possibly a lucky grab from our shelter. No sooner had that given me a sense of relief I was sucked under again.

I knew my only chance was to relax and go with the flow, hoping to hit the riverbank at some point. Unfortunately, it wasn't the bank I hit but an overhanging branch that knocked me senseless and only my desire to survive roused me to fight again. I could feel the surge of water was slowing, but it still held me in its grip, and I finally succumbed to accept my fate. Had Master known this would happen? The lights went out and I sank slowly into a place where there seemed to be peace. Maybe I would join my master again.

Suddenly there was a yank on my head as something caught my hair. For a moment, there was excruciating pain in my scalp until I surged to the surface, my lungs bursting for air. Then back under once more, and this time I couldn't stop water filling my mouth. Yet again, I was ripped from the depths and knew this must be Audric trying to save my life, and no doubt his own. The flow of water was still strong, but the worst was over; we still had a chance.

Oh, to hear that voice.

"Hold tight, Tork."

We both had some support from the meagre branch, but it all seemed fragile and helpless.

"Next corner, overhanging branches; ready," Audric spluttered optimistically.

We kicked and paddled hard towards the bank, and this time, the force and direction of the flow offered us a chance of safety. We both caught the overhang, and luck was in our favour as our float jammed into the branches holding us firm. Finally, we used our remaining strength to pull ourselves onto the riverbank. We lay there exhausted, coughing up the murderous waters and still hearing the raging river passing us by.

After a while, Audric rolled over and looked at me.

We both looked at each other nervously, and I couldn't help but say, "Is that what you meant by adventure?"

After a short pause, we both laughed out loud, knowing that we'd had a very close call. I lay there reflecting on our short journey. We had set off with very little, but now we had nothing. Audric was a real sight; hair flattened against his face and only the garment he slept in hanging from his body. My former master had made it clear there would be no going back and that we must take care of ourselves. Well, we had just about done that, but we would need even more luck to improve our fortunes.

Chapter 3

When the rain eased and the River Rede had lost its anger, we felt rested enough to make our way. It was 25 miles to Hexham, a lot for one day, but if we could get there by evening, we might find food and shelter. Audric explained there were a few farm settlements down that way, and Hexham Abbey was under construction. There should be the possibility of labouring jobs, tree felling, or working the land; enough to make a living.

After several miles along a narrow track, we hit the road we'd been aiming for, an old Roman road in poor condition after many years of neglect. We doubted it was fit enough to take all but the most robust horse and cart. However, it speeded up our journey, and the weather was warm and calm, very welcome after the rain the previous night. We had drunk well at the riverside, but now we were hungry after our exertions.

Audric guessed my thoughts. "I could just eat the hind of a roasted pig and swig a jar of good mead."

The idea made my mouth water. "Let's hope we get to Hexham in good time and the locals can see our need; otherwise, we'll need to scavenge in the dark."

We continued in this manner, with light banter and the occasional short rest, making good time. By mid-afternoon, we spotted a road sign suggesting five miles to go, and so we picked up the pace to reach our destination with daylight to spare. Our first sight of Hexham was surely the Abbey. From a distance, its prominence gave the impression it was largely complete, but hopefully, there was still work to be done.

Before we reached the landmark, we came across a farm settlement with a good range of crops and an array of cows, sheep, pigs, goats and geese. There were a few people in the fields, but in the main, it was a peaceful sight, almost idyllic. Hopefully, there would be hospitality to be had, but our appearance might not aid our hopes. There were around twenty dwellings or shelters, possibly supporting about a hundred people, probably as a farm collective.

"Let's head to that dwelling over there," suggested Audric.

"Aye," said Tork, "and you had better straighten up your Sunday best if we are not to frighten them off."

We had a good reception; the elder in the group nodded his head, gave a bit of a grin, and said, "I can see you've hit on hard times. Would you like a drink? My name's Elred." Pointing to the two younger men, he continued, "This is Canu and Gavin."

"I'm Audric, and this is Tork. We'd really appreciate a drink and maybe a bit of advice; we've had a difficult time this last day or so."

Elred turned to Gavin. "Fetch them some water and a crust of bread with cheese." The young men were still staring at me when Elred looked at Gavin again.

"Come on, get a move on."

Gavin slunk off, still staring back all the way.

Elred turned to me, "Sorry, forgive them; they haven't seen a dwarf before. For that matter, I've only met a couple in my time."

I edged forward into full view, feeling slightly less conspicuous. "Hi, it's not easy; I don't often get such a friendly reception. Where did you see these other dwarves?"

"About five years ago, up near Alnwick. I think they'd just come off a ship, though they were Britons. Nice enough company, but then they went their own way. Don't take any notice of my two boys; there'll be fine."

Audric broke in, "We're on the lookout for work and to settle somewhere until we get back on our feet."

"You might be lucky there, two families have just moved on, but there are certain ways we have here. Not unlike elsewhere, but we don't want rogues coming in and upsetting the apple cart."

Gavin returned with the food and drink and showed his lack of hospitality by placing the platter on a stool well away from us.

"Thanks," I said in a sharp voice, and Gavin jumped back as if he had been snapped at by a dog.

That put a smile on my face, and Elred laughed, then continued, "Basically, you get out what you put in. Though no one checks your labours, god forbid if you don't do a good shift. As long as you contribute to the farm's success, one of the dwellings is yours. You maintain it, but there's help if you need it. Food is prepared communally and separately; you just settle into a routine, so people around you know your preference. The brethren near the Abbey own the land and take some of the produce as payment."

We nodded our consent.

"Wonderful!" remarked Audric as he looked around, appreciating the surroundings and Elred's friendly manner.

"Finally," continued Elred, "there are eight settlements in the area around Hexham, and if the need arises, we protect our lot by forming a small armed band. Weapons and shields are hidden nearby."

Audric and I looked at each other and gave a cheerful exchange. "Thanks, that's great," said Audric. "What do we do first?"

"Canu will take you down to one of the two unoccupied dwellings, and you can settle in. Make your way to the large shelter over there when the door is open, and you see people coming and going. That's if you want to eat." Elred set to move away then turned, "Canu will also drop off day shirts and hose so you can eat in comfort. I'll introduce you to other leaders then."

Canu led us to a slightly run-down dwelling, but it was a godsend after our recent exploits. Inside there were two single bunks and a small double bunk for children. In the centre was a hearth, and alongside was space to sit and eat or pass the time of day. Perhaps not so impressive, but we thanked Canu, and he disappeared at a trot without a word.

I felt relieved to be settled. "Not bad, imagine what the other place might be like. That lad Canu seemed a bit strange, maybe shy?"

"I think he could be deaf and dumb," replied Audric. "Elred seemed to mouth to him in an exaggerated way."

The evening meal went well, and we were made very welcome by the leaders.

As the days and weeks passed by, we became part of the community. I worked in the fields and did repairs on the buildings. Canu was increasingly present and was indeed deaf, but we found ways to communicate with improvised signing. Despite my stature, Canu seemed to prefer my company to his brother's.

Audric spent a lot of time working up at the Abbey, where his skills were best suited, particularly his ability to climb ropes to assist with the completion of the roof. I preferred to keep my feet firmly on the ground. Just watching Audric moving around up there made me dizzy. This work had the advantage of earning coinage which could be useful in time away from the farming communities."

The months passed, and the leaves changed colour and began to fall off the trees. Working conditions were becoming more difficult and much colder. There was less to do in the fields, so I spent more time weatherproofing the buildings whilst work on the Abbey continued.

Then the day came I could never forget. Audric was high in the rafters of the Abbey, knocking in pegs to secure the timbers. Using a rope and pulley deck, he was easing himself from rafter to rafter. I was below, having brought him his lunch around midday. Suddenly I heard a creak. All in one movement, a rafter shifted downwards, and Audric's support fell away from under him. He yelled and made a grab for a nearby rope but missed it by inches. He slid sideways and then went into freefall. First one hand, then the other reached out, and he clung by his fingertips to a nearby joist. Below there was just a drop to what seemed like certain death. There was no easy way to get help up to Audric, and it looked as though he would only hang on a short while longer. Fear tore through my mind, and I couldn't think for the moment.

Then my head cleared, and I instinctively screamed, "Sher!"

As if in anticipation, Sher soon appeared from behind the apex of the roof and swooped in a short distance from Audric. Sher set his claws around a dangling rope, took off, hovered a few feet above Audric then lowered the rope alongside him. Audric didn't have the strength to lift himself up, so he just swung his body, let go of the joist and grabbed the rope. Then he began to fall again, but the rope went taut after a short distance. Fortunately, the rope was still linked to the pulley system, and Audric was able to lower himself to the ground. He collapsed with relief, and we ran to his aid.

High on the surrounding wall, Sher stood proudly before strutting slightly; then, he took off with a sharp squawk.

Without thinking, I whispered, "Thank you, Master," feeling deep down he was still there looking after us both.

Audric sat up, looked at everyone, then said, "Whose turn next?"

I replied, "You won't be going up there again unless I'm with you, and there is no way I'm going to even think about it."

Audric smiled. For the moment, he had no intention of contradicting me. "Let's eat that lunch of mine."

As it happens, Audric was back at work a few days later, finishing off the same job but with a harness as an additional safety measure. As the winter weather became more severe, the community went into hibernation, living off the stockpiled food. The animals were allowed to roam, but when the snow and ice took hold, it was quite normal to bring them back to shelter. This included allowing sheep into the dwellings where their warmth helped make life a little more comfortable. Keeping the hearth fire going meant restocking the timber sheds occasionally, but the hard work was welcome to keep us warm and active.

As spring approached, the daily routine of work returned. By now, Canu and I were good friends, and Audric seemed well-liked because he was friendly and hard working. Despite this, we began to have conversations about the future.

"I sense it will be very soon that Morgan will pass on his powers," Audric unexpectedly remarked one day. "This period on the farm settlement has been a welcome time for us to develop our friendship, but I'm ready to move south to places where more opportunities will present themselves."

"I'd noticed you had something on your mind in recent days," I replied, "I'll miss the friends we have made here. When were you thinking of setting off?

"We'll mention it to the community over the next few days before deciding, but not too long."

"Are you curious about the powers you will acquire?"

"Morgan only explained them in broad terms, suggesting they could influence me in subtle ways different to how he and others before him were gifted. It would be up to me to manage the powers to best protect ourselves and others."

"That must be why Master asked me not to discuss the powers I've witnessed, in case I influenced your expectations."

"In that case, let's wait and see. Maybe it will improve my cooking skills!"

"Aye, I'll second that."

Over the next few days, we thanked everyone for their wonderful friendship but explained our desire to move on. We decided to plan an early summer departure and seek horses to aid our travels. Our best opportunities were to hunt for stray, feral horses on the fells or find a breeder with a couple of low cost 'chancers'. We could never afford a well-bred horse.

We discussed this with Elred, and he directed us to an area a few miles west where packs of feral horses ran free along with small herds of wild ponies. Canu and Gavin agreed to help us as rounding up horses in the wild was no easy task. The trip was fruitful but only after several failed attempts and the horses running out of steam from teasing us to death.

We all had a good laugh, and even Gavin had a smile on his face as he asked, "Where will you go next?"

I looked at Audric, and he replied, "We'll continue south, maybe to Ripon or Eoforwic."

Canu looked sad, having guessed what was being talked about, so I put my arms around his waist and gave him a friendly punch in the ribs.

"But one day, we'll return to our friends in Hexham and have a great party."

After a bit of shadow boxing, a cheery smile returned to Canu's face.

After that, the talk went a little flat, but we had our prizes for the day: two frisky but manageable horses.

It was with these horses that we set off a few days later, well-stocked with provisions. The community gave us a good send-off as we weaved our way through the farmland and passed the abbey, where a shiver went up my spine. Audric seemed nonchalant, probably more excited about the future than the past.

Chapter 4

It was strange to see the change in Audric after just a year. He was much taller and broader in the shoulders, more upright and confident, seated there on his stead. He was clearly more conscious of his appearance, his black hair gleaming in the sunlight and cut shorter, whilst he now had the makings of an adult beard. Our clothes were plain, but Audric seemed almost regal in his attire. As for me, two score years on, I had grown my beard longer, and my skin showed a loss of youthfulness, but I felt fitter than ever after time working on the farm.

We had arrived in Hexham carrying nothing, but were now moving along astride two horses well laden with provisions. Audric, in his spare time on the farm, had made a dozen bows and numerous arrows from well-seasoned willow. Most he bartered in exchange for garments made from sheep wool and useful leather hides from the older cattle put to slaughter. I had spent time with the smithy, helping make and repair farm tools. In return, he made us two fine hunting knives. We still had coinage left over from Audric's wages for working on the Abbey, but these silver coins would have to find their use later. We knew we would reach places where society had moved on at a faster pace and coinage was more widely used.

As we pulled up for a midday break, it was clear the horses were coping well and proving a great asset. We unburdened them and fastened them to graze. I fetched some water in a leather pail from a nearby stream, and they lapped away thirstily. We enjoyed a pleasant lunch of cheese and apple sheltering from the sun under a rowan tree and reflected on our last twelve months.

"After dragging ourselves out of the floodwaters a year ago, we'd reached rock bottom, and I never imagined we'd make such good progress," I commented.

"We've done well," replied Audric. "We were made really welcome on the Hexham settlement, I'll miss them, but my mind tells me change is on the way."

"Aye, I can usually tell when you're in your contemplative mood – you go quiet and have this intense look on your face."

"Well, let's get back in the saddle and see if we can move a step closer to this change."

During the afternoon, the pathway was clear and uninterrupted, so good progress was made. We passed one small farmstead, and whilst it looked inviting, we decided to keep on the go.

"How do you feel, Tork? I feel drained. Can we set up camp for the day? I need to rest."

"Aye, it's probably the emotion of leaving our friends behind. I'll sort out a shelter if you see to the horses."

"Thanks, I'm not going to be very good company this evening."

A short time later, Audric slipped into the shelter, rolled onto his bedroll and was asleep within a few minutes. I sat down to reflect and thought about how I would miss Canu and some of the routines on the farm which gave shape to our lives. However, it was just as easy to speculate about the future, new opportunities and what might be more interesting societies.

Those we had talked to on the farm who had travelled more extensively mentioned the increasing development of small towns with permanent dwellings, workshops and market stalls, plus busy communities full of traders and craftsmen with extraordinary skills. There was talk of not just stonemasons and pottery makers but people who could fashion wonderful jewellery and clothing for those with plenty of coinage. There were inns where you could sit to drink beer, cider, mead and new wines, and stalls where you could buy food cooked over charcoal fires to eat in the street. The thought encouraged me to eat, but Audric seemed settled for the night.

As the darkness came in, I could hear a rambling conversation from the shelter and went over to check if Audric was awake, but he seemed to be in the middle of a dream. He talked as if playing the parts of different characters as though in conversation with others, but very little made real sense. I thought, *"This could be Master's doing. What must it be like inside Audric's head?"* This went on and on, but I'd always been told not to wake someone from their dreams. Anyway, I decided to bed down in the open, slightly away from Audric, to get a decent sleep. Whilst he talked, I assumed he would be fine and eventually settle down.

Despite my religious uncertainty, I said a short prayer. "Save my friend, for he has much to offer. Amen."

Surprisingly, I quickly fell asleep as if entering my own dreamland, occasionally waking but falling asleep again when all seemed well.

When I awoke in the morning sunlight, I felt refreshed and sat up to see Audric eating ravenously, as if he'd not been fed for a week.

"Morning, Tork, great day. Why did you sleep out here last night?"

"It might be something to do with you talking to yourself all night. Load of gibberish," I replied with a smile.

"Strange you should say that because my mind seems different this morning, full of possibilities I've not thought of before. It's difficult to explain at the moment, but it's as if my head is going to explode with new ideas."

I looked over at Audric and could see something I hadn't seen for over twelve months, a glaze in his eyes and a keenness of expression unmistakeably reminiscent of my Master. "Just take your time this morning, Audric; it could be a day to reflect rather than go charging on. Get your mind sorted first."

So, had Master passed away? Would Audric acquire some of his powers? It would be very weird if I was going to experience some of the things I'd seen in the past. I looked at Audric again and thought, 'maybe it's just my imagination.'

"Save some of that food for me," I said.

"Yes, sorry, I seemed to have got carried away this morning. Try this pork; it's really well flavoured. We'll have a walk along the stream before setting off again."

"Aye, that's a good idea." I wondered what the days ahead would hold and bit off a chunk of delicious meat to distract my mind from the many possibilities.

We strolled by the stream, talking about our destination, which was to be Ripon. We had heard that another large church was being erected in the town based on the design of a stone basilica seen in Rome by an Abbot Wilfrid. This had already attracted many stonemasons, glaziers and plasterers, and the work would take years. The town was developing fast and becoming a prominent centre for traders to take root and grow their businesses. Whilst religion was not our flavour, it seemed to be at the core of prosperity and well-being.

Audric suddenly stopped, "Just a moment while I try something." He took off his boots, paddled into the stream and looked down into the water rippling by. He cupped his hands in the stream then waited patiently before quickly lifting his hands out again with a good size fish.

With a big grin on his face, he announced, "Well, I never knew I could do that!"

Then he slipped the fish back into the stream and laughed.

I realised that this was a well-honed skill for some people, but, to me, it was another sign that Audric was changing. However, I decided to wait a little longer before discussing it with him.

"You'll keep the next one, I hope, then we won't grow hungry," I said.

"Sure, but I swear I've never done or seen that done before in my life. It's strange. I feel different, full of confidence that there is nothing I couldn't do."

By mid-morning, we had made good progress and reached another farmstead where a broken-down sign showed the name Stanhope. The land looked good, and the crops were growing tall. We'll call in here and see if they have any fresh produce to sell. We were met by a man and woman alongside a well-built dwelling with a child playing in the background. First impressions, they were suspicious of us but smiled nevertheless.

"Hi," called Audric, "we wondered if you have any spare food for sale? We have a few days yet before we get to Ripon. My name's Audric, and this is Tork; we've travelled from Hexham."

"I'm Dane, and this is Marcy. We can spare some cheese and a jug of broth if you have time to sit with us. There's no cost for good company. We've not seen a soul for days. The lad behind is Drake, our son."

"Thank you," said Audric. "You're very kind. We'll tie up the horses and join you."

We sat around a table outside their home and enjoyed a pleasant lunch, chatting mainly about their farm and how well it was kept. Dane said he worked hard and just hoped they could stay clear of trouble. There were only another five families on the farmland, and they'd heard of other farmsteads where the families had been forced off the land by foreigners. He mentioned having been to Ripon a year ago as they were considering moving to a more developed area, but he found it too busy and preferred the peace of the countryside. Marcy was quiet and keeping a watchful eye on her son.

"He looks a fine boy. Does he help on the farm?" I asked.

Marcy looked pleased, "Yes, he's a good lad, always on the go, though there are no children of his age on the farm. That was one reason we thought about moving."

Audric turned around and looked in the distance, a serious expression on his face. I looked but saw nothing untoward. Audric stood there as if frozen on the spot, but his eyes were agitated and searching for something.

"Get the boy inside right now; I can feel trouble coming our way. Tork, take our horses and the bows round the back of the dwelling and stay ready. Dane, you stay with me. Remain calm and don't show any concern."

His instructions were so decisive we all jumped to our tasks without question.

By the time I was in place, the sound of hooves could be heard approaching fast. Then riders came over the brow, about ten in all. They had no weapons drawn, but something didn't look right. It was difficult to know if the warriors were part of a larger band as they rode in at pace, then pulled up sharply in front of Dane and Audric.

"Can we help you?" asked Dane, with a determined voice.

"No, we'll help ourselves," laughed the one at the head of the pack. "Just keep out of the way until we're done, and no one will get hurt."

Two of the riders dismounted and walked menacingly towards the dwelling, ignoring Dane and Audric. I prepared an arrow ready to fell one of the two, but Audric stepped across the sight into the path of the two rogues. One drew a knife, but I couldn't get a clear view, so I waited. Audric stared at the assailant with intensity, and the man seemed transfixed by the glare. He fumbled somewhat, then suddenly returned his knife to its sheath, turned about and went back to his horse and led it away.

Another of the warriors followed him in a similar manner, and not a word was spoken until the leader jumped off his horse shouting, "What the hell's going on?"

He pulled his knife and was about to threaten Audric when Audric gripped his wrist in what appeared to be a vice-like grip, put a foot behind his leg and forced the man to the floor, turning the knife to his throat.

"Call your men off now," said Audric.

One man jumped off his horse and pulled his sword but got no further as my arrow went deep into his shoulder, sending him staggering back.

There was no need to call men off now as they reined their horses back a few feet.

"Enough!" shouted the man on the ground. "You have the edge."

Audric released his grip and stood back, waiting to see if there was any further reaction.

The leader stood up and offered his hand to Audric, "You'll have no further trouble from us."

Audric took the man's hand and then whispered something in the man's ear. He stared at Audric, turned, mounted his horse and rode off with his band.

Marcy and the boy came out of the dwelling, and everyone looked at Audric. Other farmers were arriving, armed with bows and knives.

Dane had hardly moved. "What happened there? I thought we were in deep trouble, or there was going to be a real fight. Why did those first two turn about?"

I went alongside Dane. "Sometimes Audric is not up for a real scrap and does it the simple way." It was easier to say that than to try and explain Audric's newfound powers. Even Audric may have been surprised. I'd find out later.

Dane accepted the vague explanation, happy that things had been resolved. "They will be back later. We'll need to be prepared."

"No, they'll not return," Audric claimed with firm assurance, "but they may lose their lives if they try again. We'll camp nearby tonight if that reassures you."

"Can we reward you in some way?" asked Dane. "Perhaps you would like to join us in a small celebration as a thank you."

The farmers took their weapons home and returned with flagons of cider and mead, followed by their womenfolk carrying bread and cuts of meat. Everyone enjoyed the break from their work, though Dane kept a watchful eye at the brow of the hill. He occasionally looked at Audric, probably thinking, 'who is this young man?' He would not be the last person to wonder in this manner.

By mid-day the following day, we were on our way again, leaving more friends behind despite our short stay. We were showered with offers of goods and food, but we could only manage a few basic provisions and two blankets that looked useful. I wanted to chat with Audric about what happened yesterday.

"Have you been practising new skills? Your actions against the band of rogues seemed remarkable."

Audric smiled. "I think we both know that this has to do with your master. At the moment, these actions are coming into my mind on the spur of the moment," he explained. "I remember what happened in the fracas, and I know that I could probably repeat it. Whilst I told you that my mind was full of possibilities, it seems that I will have to wait for situations to develop that prompt my actions. I can sense when danger is imminent, even if the risk is out of sight. When the men threatened to attack at close range, I instinctively realised I could affect their minds if I looked them directly in the eyes. When their leader closed in on me, I chose to disarm him and found I did it spontaneously at great speed; I think much faster than my usual reactions."

"You have shown yourself to be very adept so far with or without new skills. You seem to be unravelling some of the skills I saw from my master."

"You did pretty well too, Tork. That arrow was well placed; we don't want carnage unless there is no choice. We mustn't go looking for a fight just to prove our worth."

A couple of uneventful days passed, and we edged ever closer to Ripon. We started to pass more settlements and see a greater number of people on the roadside, some begging for food and others going about their daily business. The roads were generally in poor condition, and carts were taking a hammering from the ruts and rocks exposed. Our horses picked their way at a good pace, and we were soon on the edge of Ripon with an increasing number of dwellings, shelters and barns. There were many small holdings rearing low numbers of cattle, sheep and geese; barely enough to make a living, but the closer we got to the centre, the more evidence there was of some prosperity.

"Let's try the Boars Head over there; see if they have a room," suggested Audric.

The door was ajar, so we knocked hard and wandered in to see several hard backed benches and a few tables, but no one around. "Anyone in?" shouted Audric.

We heard a shuffle of feet and a middle-aged woman came into view from behind a timber wall.

"Hello, my lads, what can I do for you? Four pennies a night for a room with two bunks and two pennies for food in the early evening, and I takes your coins first each day you stay."

Audric passed a few coins to the woman, "One night will be fine. We'll let you know about the food later. Can we get a beer now?"

"Sits yourselves down there, and I'll bring it out. No extra charge."

The beer was warm and lacked much flavour, but it relieved our thirst. We were missing the friends and atmosphere of Stanhope, but surely there would be more to offer in Ripon than this cold and dank inn.

Chapter 5

We slept well despite the drab surroundings. The room contained little more than two straw-filled bunks, each with a single woollen blanket. There were no windows and just tiny amounts of light coming through cracks in the walls, but it was dry and reasonably warm.

"What's the plan today?" I asked as Audric struggled to shake off his sleepiness.

"Check the horses, then wander around Ripon."

The first thing we noticed was how busy the streets were as we rambled down what appeared to be the main thoroughfare. It was difficult to concentrate on the surroundings with the threat of bumping into people or falling over their carts, but there was a lot to interest us.

"Takes a bit of getting used to, all these people," I remarked.

Audric continued to observe. "If we are to help the people, we need to be amongst them in their everyday lives."

"Interesting the way some dwellings have opened up their frontage to display their wares."

"Yes, and notice, on the temporary stalls, the quality of the items on display. They look beyond the means of most people."

Flashy bangles and necklaces were attracting a small crowd, and the stallholder was sounding the praises of his wares. So Ripon was thriving and gave the appearance of a growing town. Further along, we saw more traders selling an array of goods:

rolls of woollen cloth, candles, pottery, pots and pans and many other extraordinary wares. My eye was taken by some oil lamps wonderfully crafted from metal, and porcelain and jewellery with intricate designs, presumably the work of the traders themselves. The appearance of some of the traders suggested several were foreigners; a couple had dark skin rarely seen up here in the north.

Unusually some of the people looking around were well-bred individuals, as distinguished by their clothing, which showed that a degree of prosperity had reached Ripon.

"Tork, I'm just having a look at the jewellery stand," Audric said, seeming more attracted to the way the jewellery was crafted rather than its value. He was asking lots of questions but made no buys.

We almost lost each other whilst engrossed in this feast of goods, but as we neared the end of the street, we met alongside a busy food market. There was a wide range of hot and cold pies, broth, cheese and meat already cooked or being turned on spits over large fire pits. We gave in to the lovely smells and bought two pies which we ate peacefully sitting on a nearby stone step to watch the crowds mingle. I turned to Audric and caught him wiping away gravy from his beard. "Not bad pies, eh? This all reminds me of my travels with my master when I saw similar levels of trading and apparent prosperity, but in these last twenty years, life has gone backwards. People have returned to the land to survive, and buildings and roads in towns and villages have fallen into ruin. Maybe prosperity is coming back into our world."

Audric pondered, "During my young years, I've only seen poverty and hardship. Certainly, in the uplands, there is little sign of this level of activity. It's good to see and adds something to people's lives. However, for those still in desperate need, the sign of such wealth will jar, and they may seek a share of this wealth by hook or by crook."

"You're right there. I've already seen a few unsavoury characters looking as if up to no good. Keep that coinage of ours out of view. It was hard-earned loafing around church spires, if you remember."

We followed the directions we'd been given to meet Abbot Wilfrid, and I reflected on the changes that had taken place in Audric. Apart from the skills passed down by my master, Audric seemed wiser and more confident in his manner. I had no doubt the abbot would be interested in employing someone like him.

We continued our way to the old church, which showed against the skyline. As we approached, it was clear the old church was about to be demolished, presumably to make way for a new one. We had heard that Abbot Wilfrid had been to Rome and seen wonderful stone-built basilica, grander than anything he had ever seen before. He received wealth, ideas and the loan of some highly-skilled builders to return to Ripon and build a church in the style of these great buildings, all in the name of promoting the Catholic religion in our country. The churches in Europe controlled the land and used it ruthlessly to manage the people who either feared or supported the church and exchanged their labour for the right to farm the land. Whilst this was harsh, it was difficult to overturn, and many accepted the way of life because it brought them a degree of certainty in their lives. There was also increasing pressure and hardship from the controlling nobilities in each kingdom, plus the occasional feuding between the different tribes within the kingdoms. So, between the church and the nobility, there was little freedom for those working the land to make a decent living.

My conversations with Audric showed me that he understood this but felt it was best to work within the power struggle and look for new opportunities for change as time went on. This reflected what I had seen in my master. He knew he could not change society just with his mystical ways but only by working to influence the people in positions of power.

We stood by the site looking for someone who might be in charge, but everyone seemed intent on rigging ropes to pull down part of the old church.

Then, from behind us, someone called, "Can I help you?"

We turned to face a middle-aged man with a ruddy complexion typical of one who worked outdoors in all conditions. "Hi, my name is Audric, and this is Tork. We are interested in talking to Abbot Wilfrid."

"The abbot only comes to the site occasionally now that the old church is to come down. A magnificent new church is to be built on the same plot. It could take years. Would you like to labour on the site, or is it some religious matter you need to discuss?"

Audric responded, "Well, we are interested in the building work and could do some labour which is good for everyone's soul, but I have in mind something a bit more than that."

"Hi, well, I'm the gang-leader; you might talk with me first."

I could see that Audric wasn't quite sure if this was the person he wanted to try and influence. "I have a reference here from our work in Hexham on the new church there. Probably not as grand as planned here, but I have developed certain skills that could help your progress."

"How's your writing and reading?" he probed.

"Pretty good," said Audric. "I can show you later if you give me something to write on or some words to read."

Audric had his attention, and the man looked at him curiously. "You must have read our thoughts before coming here. The abbot likes to keep a tight control of all comings and goings and was thinking of using one of his brethren, but he is reluctant to take them away from their religious ways. It could be worth you seeing him. If you come back when the sun goes down, I'll take you to see the abbot. Note he spends most of his time in Eoforwic now the church is being rebuilt, so don't be late. If he's interested, he'll tell you all about the job he has in mind. Now, I have to get on. My name is Angus."

He shook hands and set off to the old church as part of a side wall came crashing down under the pull of the ropes.

"Did you know about this before we came here?" I sounded at Audric.

"Sometimes fate deals a poor hand, but this time we may have been lucky. Let's not count our chickens before they hatch, though. Let's have another wander around."

"I think you've already counted your chickens," laughed Tork.

"We will see, Tork, we will see," said Audric with a glimmer of a smile on his face.

As the sun came down and the cool air swirled around, we approached the site where most of the church now lay in ruins.

We could see Angus in the distance giving out instructions. On seeing us, he walked over and pointed. "This way."

We walked about a mile to the outskirts of town, passing a few areas of farmland that looked to be well managed before coming upon a small stone and timber dwelling. Angus knocked hard on the door, and shortly someone came to the door. "I've come to see Abbot Wilfrid, and he may want to see these two."

The monk retreated then returned, asking us to follow him.

When we saw Abbot Wilfrid, he showed no surprise in our presence, which was odd, and he gave us a pleasant smile.

"Please, sit down."

We sat at a small table in a room lit by several candles.

"How can I help you?"

Angus related our earlier conversation and passed over the note given to him. The abbot passed Audric some parchment and a quill and ink. "Write down what you see in the room."

Audric paused and looked around, then started to write in what seemed a fluent manner. After several lines could be seen, he passed the record back to the abbot.

"This is very good, and you added a bit of Latin at the end. Where did you learn this? It is usually only someone who has spent time in the church who knows Latin, or for that matter can write."

Audric didn't waver, "My parents, and then my guardians taught me many things about the land, building and how to survive in life. Later I spent time with a wonderful man called Morgan, who developed my scholarly skills."

"You also speak well and with such confidence. That's quite something for such a young man."

"Thank you," replied Audric modestly.

"I could definitely use someone like you. As time goes on, the work will become more complex, and you'll need to adapt. There's a need to record everything that comes in and, along with Angus, ensure that all materials remain secure. Similarly, the craftsmen and labourers must have their work written down. You will be paid at three-quarters of a craftsman's wage and will report to Angus on site but to me once a week if I am not in Eoforwic. I have a sense you want such a job, but what do you say?"

"You are very generous, Sir, and you are correct. I would love the job and the opportunity to learn. My only other request is that Tork is also taken on with me. He is a very capable worker, and I would use him to help with the protection of the site. There may be times when we need someone around both day and night."

"Very wise, I can see we are going to get on fine. Angus, please show them to their accommodation. Introduce them to the craftsmen and their labourers. Ensure they understand Audric's role and that he has my full support."

We set off back down the road and Angus said, "If you have a place to live in Ripon, then that's fine, but we have acquired a few dwellings through the church following some of the brethren being moved to Eoforwic. It's very plain; each room is for one person, which seems to suit most of the workers. We eat in the community shelter, where the women prepare our food. It's all free and provided by the church, though be aware the church gets the produce from the farms in the area as payment to live on the land. When times get tough, that can cause tension with the farmers."

The accommodation was very simple but let in good daylight and allowed us to mix with some of the craftsmen and labourers. A lot of labour came from the surrounding farms and was an alternative to providing produce from the farm. The hours worked by us all were very long, and the work was strenuous at times. We were allowed Sunday off as a benefit of working for the church, but we were encouraged to attend church services in the open or the communal area. Many of us took the opportunity to rest or go for a short walk in the country, whilst the local farm labourers returned to their farmland to work and be with their families.

Audric made my role clear. I was to help with the building work when time allowed, but my main role was to keep a keen eye on all workers and ensure no materials went missing. We were to watch out for each other as the nature of our work would be resented by some who saw small amounts of pilfering as acceptable. Our aim was to intervene before matters became too serious and avoid having to lay off workers whose numbers were sorely needed. Despite the nature of our work, we got on well with the workers, and we were not the ones forcing the pace to get the work done as quickly as possible. That job lay with Angus, who was both hated and respected all in one breath.

Most of the time, the work ran smoothly, but this was a very long and intensive task, so problems were always going to occur.

"You'd think you've been doing this job for years," Angus commented as he looked over Audric's shoulder. "Those sketches are works of art."

"It makes the work all the more enjoyable to receive such praise," replied Audric.

"Your efforts also allow me more time with the men on site. They're just the same, require a bit of encouragement."

Tork was listening in the background, "Whilst you two have been using your brains, my muscles have grown twofold, and I creak every morning when I get out of my bunk."

"You set a great example to the men," retorted Angus. "Let's go have a beer whilst Audric sees the abbot."

I rarely attended Audric's meetings with the abbot, but they seemed to go well, and the abbot was happy with the progress.

Twelve months on, the foundations were in place, and the lower sections of the wall were built. Several accidents had occurred, but the worst was a broken foot, the rest, nasty bruises and cuts leading to a few days off work. Apparently, the building work was on time, and early impressions were good.

It was a pleasant sunny day when Audric and I sat a short distance from the site, eating our usual lunch of bread and cheese.

"It's been a long, hard year, Tork, and you deserve a lot of praise for keeping us both safe and sane. Sometimes it seems difficult to keep going, but you're always there to chivvy me on and encourage me to get through the day. I might have acquired some wonderful skills, but you have the greater staying power."

"I'm just keeping an eye on you in case you decide to go climbing again. Apart from that, it seems to be going well, but we'll need to be more aware this coming year as there will be a far greater range of building goods to watch over."

"You may be right, Tork, but I have graver concerns about the future. Did Morgan have premonitions or sense future danger?"

"Aye, over many years, he had what he called visions and seemed to anticipate threats coming our way. Have you experienced something?"

"These last couple of days, I've had a repeated premonition suggesting the tribes throughout Mercia are gathering and tracking towards Northumbria."

"I would trust your instincts. At least we need to be prepared."

"Unless the nobility of Northumbria rally its tribes and warns its farmers, we could be overrun. Eoforwic is well protected, according to Abbot Wilfrid, and those who rallied may be able to come to our aid, but we are not well organised here. I don't wish to fight, but there may be no choice unless we accept being pushed back north. I need to see the abbot and make a suggestion. This could be very dangerous, and we'll need to be more careful than ever."

I sighed, "Just when I thought we were settled, but if it means time away from this back-breaking work, then I, for one, won't grumble. What have you got in mind?"

"I'll let you know soon enough, but let me sleep on it. First, let's check the site carefully this afternoon as we might be away for a week or two."

We double-checked the works, and everything seemed in order. I pondered what Audric was up to, but as usual, it would all become clear when he was ready. Building churches was one thing; war was tragically far more onerous, as my past experiences reminded me.

Chapter 6

It is better that I, Audric, pick up the story at this point as I began to be affected in significant ways by Morgan's transfer of powers, some of which I never fully explained to Tork at the time.

The nights before we went to see Abbot Wilford about our concerns for insurgence by the Mercian army, I experienced my first premonition and the start of an internal dialogue that challenged my reason to live. I usually slept well, and Tork would often be up well before me, but that night, I felt unsettled as soon as I lay on my bunk. It was not unusual for me to daydream and think about the days ahead, but this became far more disturbing as I drifted off.

"What makes you think you can change society? You didn't even try to save your parents."

"But… I tried for years. I haven't given up."

"Morgan has given you powers; you mustn't waste them. You have the chance to rule the people around you and impose your authority."

"Maybe, but it seems fairer to help people control their own lives."

"You're young; you will see that only the powerful survive and lead a full life."

"But that's why I have the powers to help overcome the evil that exists in the world."

"You mix up evil with leadership and authority."

No!… I'm getting confused; that's enough.

"You must be strong. The weak must be allowed to flounder, and you can build your empire around the survivors in life. This may be the quickest way to find your parents again."

"Enough, ENOUGH, I say."

"The Mercian army stands ready to strike in a matter of days. You have the power to influence the battle and become a man of great power. It doesn't matter which side you chose; just make sure you're amongst the winners."

"Some of what you say makes sense, but no, it's not my way in life."

"Don't be weak; you'll regret it."

"You are not the real me."

"Then who am I if not you? You have the world before you."

"But…"

I woke up in a great sweat from what seemed like the real world into a dark reality. Did I really know how I might use Morgan's powers?

I was quiet over breakfast, but that was not unusual to Tork, who was used to my contemplative silences. Tork had been amazingly supportive on our travels, and we had a great rapport, but at this stage, I didn't feel inclined to share my inner thoughts from last night. I must confess I was still confused.

We were up early the following morning and made straight for Abbot Wilfrid's dwelling. I wasted no time explaining my thoughts but avoided directly mentioning my premonition.

"We're sorry to disturb you so early, but I wanted to catch you before you go back to Eoforwic. As you know, the insurgents from Mercia have made several forays over the last year into Northumbria, wrecking or stealing goods or weapons. However, they have made no real attempt to gain land suggesting this is a deliberate ploy to weaken our resolve. I have a very overactive mind and strongly sense an attack is coming soon; we need to be better prepared. If we are to defend this challenge, we need to find out more about their plans and their capabilities. I'm proposing that someone should get amongst the Mercians and spy on their activities to discover their plans."

Abbot Wilfrid contemplated for a moment or two. "Your ideas seem somewhat speculative, but on the other hand, we cannot ignore the prospect of war. This is very unusual, and I'm not the leader of the Northumbrian tribes, but these matters have been raised in Eoforwic by the overlords sent to protect us there. I travel there later today, so join me and explain your thoughts to them."

By late morning, we were all on our way to Eoforwic: Abbot Wilfrid and his assistant, and Tork and I. The way was busy, and at times we had to take the horses around carts carrying goods in each direction, but we were travelling light and made good progress. We took a short break for lunch but pushed on, hoping to make Eoforwic by evening. We talked a little about the progress of the church in Ripon, but generally, we were quiet and keen to get to our destination.

Suddenly a group of riders broke out onto the woodland track, clearly having waited in ambush. It seemed unlikely we were their specific target, but they were armed like warriors, and my concerns heightened sharply. They surrounded us in a menacing way but didn't make an immediate attack.

I turned to Tork and whispered, "Stay calm, no weapons yet."

The apparent leader decided Abbot Wilfrid was our spokesman and rode up alongside him whilst keeping a weathered eye on Tork and me. "So, man of God, where are you bound?"

"To Eoforwic to study and pray," answered the abbot.

"And you go there often?"

"A few times a month."

"And it's a busy place, is it?"

By now, my senses were working overtime, and I realised they were Mercian soldiers and likely seeking information about the Northumbrian defences in the town.

"*Abbot, take care with your answers*," I thought, staring at Abbot Wilfrid, who looked startled to receive my advice.

However, he regained his composure and replied, "It gets busy on market days and when they hold festivals."

"How many men protect the town?"

"Very few, there hasn't been the need since warring stopped years ago."

"We're looking to join the Northumbria army," the man lied.

"*They're Mercians*," I warned the abbot, who was even more taken aback, turning towards me with a questioning expression as if my first thoughts had been an aberration.

"The last I heard, they were up near Alnwick," he countered with his own lie.

"Then we wish you good day, man of God. Sorry for the intrusion."

The warriors rode off the way we had come, and once out of sight, Abbot Wilfrid turned to me, looking quizzically. "Was that voice I heard in my head yours, Audric?"

"Think of it more that you anticipated my thoughts in a moment of danger."

Tork smiled but stayed silent.

The abbot pursed his lips as if to speak again but paused, and so I quickly took the opportunity to try and change the subject.

"Shall we move on before the dark comes in?"

We turned to go, but I sensed Abbot Wilfrid would have more questions later.

There was still plenty of light as we approached a gate to the city where there was a cursory check on our group, and we entered a world even busier than Ripon. The buildings were more substantially built, and the town looked what it was: a major monument to its roman past. A street market was closing down for the day, and traders were packing their carts to go home. The substantial stone walls gave the city enormous protection, and large sections of the old Roman fort remained and its thoroughfares.

Whilst most buildings were built of timber, a few were erected in stone, more relics of Roman times. It was towards one of these that we headed and were met by a group of monks who took our horses and led us into the building. It seemed to be a religious centre, and its importance was soon realised when we were introduced to a man in distinctive clothing that set him apart from the others present.

Abbot Wilfrid bowed slightly in reverence and said, "This is Archbishop Theodore travelled up from Canterbury and temporarily residing in Eoforwic."

Despite his eminence, he bowed in return, "These are the two you have talked about so enthusiastically. Welcome to Eoforwic. What brings you here?"

Abbot Wilfrid intervened, "Our matter is not religious other than it will protect our interests throughout Northumbria. We will need to see the overlords to discuss certain matters relating to the security of the kingdom. When we have done that, I will report back."

"In that case, you will dine with me tonight, and we will talk about the progress with the church in Ripon," said the archbishop. "I look forward to seeing you all later."

Abbot Wilfrid showed us around the ecclesiastical building, and we saw things we had never seen before. Monks were working in large numbers, diligently reproducing manuscripts and inscriptions for books; some of the originals apparently hundreds of years old and in different languages. The writing was beautifully done but must have been very laborious and time-consuming. We saw a room given over to the storage and display of such books, and whilst we had heard about libraries, neither of us had ever been in such a place. In fact, I had seen very few books in my lifetime, so scarce was reading and writing amongst the people. Some monks were simply reading as part of their studies, and others appeared to be debating their religious views. What struck us was the degree of calm and the obvious contrast between their lives and what we called normality. Many people had converted to Christianity and pursued it with vigour, but most were still pagans out in the farmlands of Britain. It was hard to imagine how the different ways could unite.

I picked up a manuscript and was amazed that I could read line after line of Latin. I knew I had received some of Morgan's knowledge, but I was astounded at the extent. I'd written a few words for the abbot but had never seen such scripts before. Even more amazingly, I could understand the meaning of the words, and as I read further, I became absorbed by the content of what I was reading. I put the manuscript down, and we headed out into the sunny courtyard. I wondered how this might change my life and what I could learn in time.

The evening meal was relaxing and a pleasant change from our crowded surroundings back in Ripon. The conversation eventually came round to the concerns regarding the insurgents from Mercia, and clearly, the archbishop had been briefed by the abbot.

"We have two hundred armed men under two overlords, Aldren and Oldred. Aldren is the most powerful and can call on a further two thousand fighting men from the main tribes in Northumbria. He is under the rule of King Ecgfrith of Northumbria, but Aldren yields great power. For the moment, they will fight together against the might of King Wulfhere, who has ruled Mercia with ruthless determination and has already taken control of lands south of Mercia. Whatever your plans, take great care."

"I hope to use neither knife nor sword but wile and wit," I suggested. "I will try to leave the fighting to those that feel the need and are ready to sacrifice their lives, but I will not stand there and be slain without defending myself. With Tork alongside me, we are a formidable pair."

Abbot Wilfrid smiled, "I have seen the resilience in your work and have heard of some of your exploits before arriving in Ripon, so I have faith in your endeavours. We will see Aldren tomorrow. A message was sent to him earlier, and he will see us in the morning. The tribes camp about a mile away along the river."

After an evening of dining in great comfort, we retreated to our bunks. I slept well, relieved not to suffer the disturbing dreams of the previous night.

After a light breakfast of milk and oats, we travelled along the river in the morning mist, soon seeing the tops of tents ahead, and we were met by a small group of armed men on horseback. They seemed to be expecting us and just turned and pointed the way. We were led to the largest of the shelters and asked to follow one of the men inside. Whatever our vision of an overlord might have been, the two men before us did not fail to meet our image.

One stood to a great height and introduced himself, "I'm Aldren, and this is Oldred; you must be Audric and Tork. Good morning, Abbot; it's a pleasure to see you again. How can we help you?"

Abbot Wilfrid began, "This young man here belies his youth and shows qualities of leadership that could be very useful. I have had faith in Audric since I first met him over a year ago, and he has met all my expectations. He strongly believes the Mercian army are readying for war, and he can aid our cause. I'll let him speak."

"What draws you to our cause?" interrupted Aldren.

"I lost my parents to warring invaders when I was eleven and have had to mature quickly. I don't look to fight battles, but I can see that there can be fewer losses if the risks are reduced, hence my desire to get involved. You don't seem intent on war like the Mercians, and perhaps there is a more peaceful solution than an all-out war on this occasion."

"And what are you proposing?" continued Aldren.

"The Mercians are only days away from our borders, and I feel more information on their strength and movements would be a great help. Tork and I are prepared to infiltrate their ranks and find out information to your advantage."

Oldred came forward, "If I met you in battle, I would think to swat you like a fly and crush your body to a pulp, but I sense that I would be making a big mistake in underestimating you. However, you probably know little of our tribes and how we can mobilise."

"True, but because of my youth, I'm likely to be underestimated by the enemy."

Aldren looked across and was about to speak but paused as I caught his gaze. He shook his head slightly then looked around. "I'm somewhat sceptical of your motives, but you seem very genuine. I don't see that we have anything to lose and perhaps a lot to gain. You have our agreement. If you are not back within a week, we will prepare for all-out war, but in any case, there is reason for us to be on alert. We will have an army by the time you return. You can have any weapons or goods you want, and we wish you all the best. I'm sure Abbot Wilfrid will pray for you. Take care."

As we returned to town, Tork whispered, "That seemed a little easy. Did you influence Aldren's decision?"

"Maybe a little," I replied with a slight glaze in my eyes. "I would have gone ahead with my plan anyway, but it will be better this way."

"You remind me of Master more each day."

Chapter 7

I was enjoying being back on the road, and I think it was the same for Tork. Since our early days together, I rarely thought of Tork's stature unless onlookers shouted out comments. He was good at deflecting any offence felt, which avoided unnecessary conflict. Whilst I was experiencing youthful growth, Tork had changed little. His rugged looks and muscular upper body, whilst mounted on his stead, made him look every bit the mighty warrior. His presence reassured me as we rode down to Elmet, an area bordering Mercia, which Northumbria had retaken some years ago. I felt this was a natural area for the enemy to pass through again to regain Elmet and move on towards Eoforwic. The attractions of Elmet were obvious with its rivers and fertile land and its central position.

We took a sheltered spot well hidden from view and estimated we were some five miles from the border. From now on, we had to be extra careful and watch our every step, so the horses were tied up alongside our camp, and we added additional camouflage to hide from view.

"Time for a little action, Tork. Sher, come."

I put my arm out, then suddenly Sher appeared from behind us and landed on the leather strap around my hand. I put Sher onto a branch and then started to arrange twigs on the ground and finally pointed to the sky and to different parts over the land into Mercia. Sher took off and soared majestically into the sky and slowly diminished into the distance to seek out the enemy position.

"Sher will return at dawn," I stated, "and if the Mercians are out there, we will have our first advantage over them. Let's relax for the moment and enjoy a good night's sleep; we may not get many in the coming days."

Dawn arrived, the sun began to rise, and we had prepared for our task ahead. Sher arrived quickly out of the trees where he must have spent the night and settled on a low branch near the two of us. He squawked several times and then took off, flying to a tree in the distance. We followed his route, and this was repeated many times until mid-afternoon when Sher came to rest and this time made no attempt to fly on but hovered just above the ground with a stick in his beak. He came back to earth and placed the stick down before strutting at one end of the stick; then he flew off, his task done.

"Tork, it's time to split up for a while. I'm going to set off in the direction Sher has indicated, and I want you to follow at a good distance with the horses. When I have found the enemy campsite, I'll retrace my steps to find you. Don't get too close, but stay close enough to see trouble if it comes in behind me."

"Take a knife," suggested Tork, "and a bit of food in case we get bogged down; it might take some time. Use the knife to dig a marker if you change direction, though don't worry too much. I'm experienced in tracking; you're not the only one with special skills!"

"That's great. If it gets dark, I'll return even if I've not found their camp."

The heightened risk of danger stimulated my mind, and I could sense the enemy were not far away in what felt like large numbers.

I set off as if already in the hunt, moving quickly across the land, hopefully with Tork following on behind in case I ran into trouble. I soon picked up rumbling noises and then distant shouts and almost tumbled into the Mercian camp in my enthusiasm.

Without doubt, this was an army preparing for war. I passed my eyes over the camp several times, and my vision seemed to capture the events as permanent memories. I retreated the way I had come and could sense Tork nearby and that he could probably see me even though I could not see him.

After tracking back for a short while, Tork appeared out of nowhere on horseback. "So, what did you find?" he asked.

"Good and bad news. I've found the enemy just a short distance away, camped by a river, but the bad news is that it looks as though they are gathering to make an invasion. Even now, fresh armed men are arriving, swelling the numbers. I would say at least three, maybe four thousand men. They seem well-resourced, with many carts full of goods and several hundred horses. I can't be sure, but I think that quite a few are straight off the fields and may not be trained or even willing fighters."

Tork recalled, "Remember the archbishop mentioned that Aldren could muster around two thousand armed men, but how quickly? And the Mercians would still outnumber us nearly two to one. Not good odds on an open battlefield."

"Well, that is why we are here - to see if we can change things in our favour. We'll rest up for the night and then consider our next move, which may be the riskiest part of our task."

I was up early and keen to see what Tork thought of my plan to enter the Mercian camp. I rummaged in my backpack and pulled out a dark brown garment that I planned to use to masquerade as a monk.

I donned the disguise and walked over to rouse Tork. "Do I look the part, Tork?"

"Aye, not bad, but maybe you look a bit young for a monk."

"Possibly, but I've spent quite a bit of time with the abbot and the monks in Ripon and understand their ways. I'll pass myself off as a novice monk travelling from Lincoln to Lindisfarne on a pilgrimage. Even though King Wulfhere of Mercia is seeking to spread his power, the abbot tells me he is a committed Christian, contrary to his father's paganism years ago, so I hope we will receive a warm welcome."

"Based on what you're saying, I'll be alongside you, but I'm not sure I'd make a passable monk. How will that work?"

"You'll act as my servant, and I'll say you were sent with me to look after my welfare on this long journey. Such long pilgrimages are common for monks to show their dedication to God and learn humility."

"Humility," Tork retorted. "We might need a lot of that if we are not to lose our heads."

"I'll do all that I can to ensure that doesn't happen but watch my back as some may be suspicious of my presence and others still support the heathen habits."

As we rode towards the Mercian camp, we agreed on a fictional story of our journey from the south. Approaching the perimeter, my stomach began to churn even though I may have looked calm and felt every bit a monk. There were other riders arriving at the camp, and our appearance did not hold a threat to this vast army of men. We were allowed to ride unhindered until reaching the central area, and at that point, several men took an interest in our presence.

"Let's dismount," I suggested, "it looks less intimidating. We'll walk over to the shelter and pretend we need food."

By now, there were four armed guards walking straight up to us, and they looked hard at us, Tork drawing the usual scrutiny. The most prominent guard eventually spoke.

"You don't look like fighting men, so what brings you here?"

I lowered my head in deference, "Excuse us for intruding, we take the road that God intends, but sometimes we make a wrong turning." That seemed to amuse the guards. "If you could spare a little food, that would be very welcome, and then we will be on our way."

The guard looked around, "Fasten your horses over there and come with me."

We did as asked and then followed him into the large shelter that was, as expected, an eating place. There was a large hearth where a couple of men were cooking a roast pig and had pots on the boil. The smell was appealing, and the guard pointed to a makeshift seat, "You don't look as though you eat much but take care; we have many mouths to feed."

I thought to take advantage and ask the numbers but decided it was too obvious at this point. "We really appreciate your kindness, and in return, we will pray for you all."

"My name is Ulloch," said the guard who seemed to have warmed to us. "Our king, Wulfhere, is a keen Christian, though I can't say that for many of the men here. Stay there, and I'll get someone to bring you food. I'll see if the king is interested in meeting you."

As Ulloch walked away, Tork whispered, "So far so good, but what do we do now?"

"Let's enjoy our food and pray thanks to God," I replied.

We sat peacefully for a good while and appreciated the hot food provided. Ulloch reappeared, "The king would like to see you both. Follow me."

As we exited the shelter and walked across the field, I looked around. There were certainly a few thousand men and a lot of weaponry on display. Archers were practising both near and long-range, and the thought of a volley of arrows cascading down was a frightening thought. Overall, it was more a scene of rest, but with such numbers, it could only be a short time before the invasion of Northumbria would take place. King Wulfhere came upon us suddenly as we turned around the side of a small tent. There he was, sitting on a straw bale, peeling an apple with a large knife. He was middle-aged and very stocky; his hair was almost white, and he had bright green eyes that locked on us immediately. He stayed seated but pointed to another nearby bale, and we sat opposite the king, still under his intense gaze.

"You seem very young to be a monk and travelling around in the middle of nowhere. Where have you come from?"

I maintained eye contact and answered, "My name is Audric, and I am a novice monk. I was brought up in the Order from a young age after my parents were killed. I have learnt many scholarly matters, and the Order thought it was time for me to see more of the world, hence a pilgrimage from Lincoln to Lindisfarne. Glancing at Tork, I explained his role as my servant. The king did not seem overly convinced, but before he could say more, I surprised him by asking if he would like Mass to be taken. The great Wulfhere, the King of Mercia, was certainly taken aback but only took a moment to agree. I stood, and the king kneeled before me. Tork appeared dumbfounded by what was happening. My heart was in my mouth whilst I conducted the Mass in Latin. It seemed an age before the king rose and took back control, nodding for me to be seated. This exchange clearly altered the king's view of us as his questioning changed in tone.

"Have you had a good journey so far?"

"We have made good progress," I replied, "and met kind people on our way. I think we have strayed off our intended route, but that is not of great concern as long as we get to Lindisfarne in the course of time."

"It may be best if you make rapid progress to your destination and remain there for some time," said the king. "Do not linger on your way, especially in Eoforwic, and you should be safe enough, but if my men come upon you again, mention that you are protected by the King of Mercia. I will provide my seal for your protection and one of my pendants to display if trouble arrives quickly. Be ready to leave tomorrow morning, and we will set you off in the right direction. You seem a remarkable young man, Audric; I wish you well in the world. Ulloch will see you have a spot to camp for the night."

"Thank you for your kindness, and we appreciate your guidance. All we hope for is peace in our lives."

King Wulfhere stood and gestured that the audience was over, "Thank you for taking Mass it has helped me this day to reaffirm my faith."

Ulloch led us out and back to our horses and showed us where to camp for the night. Whilst Tork had stayed silent during the encounter, he was worn out by the tension of our engagement with the king.

"I hope you have no further plans for the night; perhaps giving a church service to the entire army?"

"Tork, you said nothing and played your part perfectly. We have learned a lot even without asking questions that might have given our game away. They have a force of about three thousand men, and maybe a third are not fully trained but taken from the fields to swell their numbers. We have their location, and they are heading for Eoforwic and will most certainly be no more than a day or so behind us. Wulfhere is strongly supportive of the Christian faith and so is unlikely to raid the city of Eoforwic directly but may look to blockade the place and seek its surrender. Despite his religious faith, he is clearly one who seeks power and will be ruthless in dealing with the nobility in Northumbria. If the Mercians do try to enter Eoforwic, they have a massive task on their hands despite their numbers. Before leaving their midst, we have one more task that I hope will slow them down. You're very good with horses, Tork, so I hope you'll accept the task I have in mind. On this occasion, I will watch your back."

I explained my plan, and in the deep of night, with clouds blanking out the moonlight, we crept from our tent and made our way towards the horses. As we got closer, all seemed calm, and there were no guards on patrol. These horses were for pulling the carts and numbered about sixty. I hid behind a tree, and Tork continued in amongst the horses, stroking and calming them with the tone of his voice. He withdrew the bottle of potion I'd given him and found several open-topped metal tanks containing water, and as suggested, Tork poured a few drops into each tank. Then he led one horse to the water, and the others followed. Tork quietly moved away, and we returned to our tent. I had explained that the potion would not harm the horses but make them idle or sleepy the following day. This would be an action not readily blamed on us and therefore should not raise any suspicion. Hopefully, it would slow the progress of the Mercian army and allow us time to return to Eoforwic and make further plans.

We rose early to prepare our packs as the sun came over the hillside, and Ulloch joined, us passing on a script showing the king's seal and a pendant holding the royal colours. As we rode through the camp, we observed the cart horses, some lying on the floor sleeping and others looking restless and uncertain in their movement. As yet, this had not raised concern amongst their handlers.

Once well clear of the camp, there was a sense of relief, but we kept up a steady pace and didn't talk much until we took a rest around mid-morning. The return journey to Eoforwic would take a day or so but maybe a couple of days longer for the Mercian army.

Tork expressed his relief. "I'm glad to be away from the Mercian camp, but the thought that they will be following us shortly is frightening. There is going to be a blood bath soon, and no one will be the winner."

"I've been lucky to avoid war," I reflected, "but I can visualise the carnage, and it won't end with just one battle if Wulfhere succeeds. We could walk away from all this and seek peace elsewhere and let the overlords grind each other into the ground. I set off from Eoforwic convinced of our cause, but now I am a little confused. I feel an allegiance to Northumbria because I have spent my life there, but it could quite easily be the Northumbrians attacking Mercia. Where does it end?"

Tork sighed, "The need for power seems to be ingrained with some people, and it leads them into insane actions to acquire a bit more land. The ones that suffer the most are the peasant farmers who simply want to live in peace but get driven off the land, and even worse get called to arms in futile battles."

"What we know for certain, Tork, is that all hell will let loose very soon unless something changes. Let's move on; my mind is working overtime again."

We set off with even more urgency, but I spoke little whilst we journeyed on, the sun rising high in the sky. We reached a small group of settlements in a place called Tadcaster, the name etched on a stone plinth, as we approached a river that seemed to have a manageable ford to cross. There was a small timber church and several dwellings, but no one in sight. We unloaded the horses and led them to the water's edge, where they guzzled thirstily. I stood in the monk's garment, looking down at the cool water, then slipped off the robe and jumped in the water. There was a strong flow to the river, so I allowed myself to drift down to the ford where I was able to stand and keep balance.

I scrambled out of the water and made for my pack. "I can't wear that robe a moment longer." I pulled out my usual clothes and re-dressed. "The water has cleared my mind, and I have a few ideas that may help our cause, but for the moment, we must move on. The people of Northumbria are at grave risk of losing their lives."

We crossed the ford and determined we would be back in Eoforwic by evening. A couple of the locals watched from a distance, and I wondered how they would react when the Mercian army approached. Almost certainly, they would run for their lives and look to hide in the woods nearby. Hopefully, Wulfhere would not order a plunder of the settlements.

Our progress was good, and I halted and said we would rest for a short while, but to be ready for travel and possibly a difficult journey back to Eoforwic. The wind had been swirling around since our stop in Tadcaster, and now the sky was darkening, a complete contrast to the morning's sunshine. This was just what might heed our cause, but the atmosphere needed a little encouragement. I walked a short distance away from Tork to quote a few words.

"Sky as grey, rain so weak, let forth your hell and hit your peak."

"It's time to go; ensure the packhorse is held tight," I announced.

Tork climbed on his stead, "Looks like a storm is due. It could be a nasty ride into Eoforwic."

"You might say that, Tork, but what could be worse than the rage behind us?"

Tork bent forward as the wind and rain began to strengthen and shouted, "This will be a bit more invigorating than your swim."

Our progress slowed, and our direction of travel became more difficult to determine, but we estimated that we would still reach Eoforwic before dark.

However, the wind had strengthened and the rain was now heavy and incessant, so we dismounted and walked to protect the horses that were struggling in the muddy conditions. We continued for some time at a very slow pace until we decided it would be better to wait out the storm. I unpacked the horses and tied them up whilst Tork improvised a shelter for us to stand under.

"The army won't be going anywhere fast if this torrent continues," shouted Tork, "and the ford will be impossible to cross whilst in flood."

He turned to me about to confirm his revelation but realised that, once again, he'd been slow to assess the situation. He laughed, and this time, I peered through the curtain of rain and smiled.

The rain eased slightly, so we resumed our trek to Eoforwic and soon picked up a more manageable road where we remounted and were able to ride slowly for the remainder of our journey. There was very little light as we entered the gate, but there were several guards who asked our business. Two of them escorted us to the abbot's residence with the rain continuing unrelentingly. As we were invited into Abbot Wilfrid's home, I realised our task was far from over.

Chapter 8

We were allowed to wash and given dry clothing before being taken to see the abbot, who expressed his happiness to see us safely returned. He was keen to hear our news but explained that he had sent for Aldren and Oldred, and they would be here soon.

"The storm has hit us badly," he continued, "and the River Ouse has flooded at several points, making many fields like bogs."

The abbot's servant knocked and entered the room, and the two overlords followed him in, bowing briefly to the abbot.

Aldren spoke with urgency. "You must have grave news to travel in such weather and considerable resolve to find your way back. Did you have any success?"

I spelt out our discoveries. "We've seen Wulfhere's forces, and they amount to about three thousand men, mostly well-armed. We saw about five or six hundred horses, and their provisions seemed plentiful. They're definitely heading through Elmet and on to Eoforwic and, but for a few interventions, could have been at our doorstep tomorrow. Depending on the army you can muster within the walls, I don't think they can breach the defences with their numbers without taking many losses attempting to scale the walls or break through the gates. However, if they lay siege, we should be well resourced whilst they will have dwindling stocks."

Aldren shuffled and put a hand to his sword hilt as if ready for battle, "You have done well. Did you catch sight of Wulfhere?"

"Just a little," Tork whispered.

I quickly explained, "What Tork means is that we infiltrated the camp as religious folk and were well received. Like you, Wulfhere is a committed Christian, and the king was interested in our pilgrimage from Lincoln to Lindisfarne."

Oldred broke in, "You seem a bagful of tricks. I hope you don't stumble under the weight."

"We have been careful rather than heroic," I explained, "but I hope our efforts can avoid unnecessary loss of life."

"We now have a thousand men in and around the town," confirmed Aldren, "and a similar number on their way in the next few days. We can also rely on recruits from the nearby settlements if they wish us to defend their land. When the storm settles, we will send out scouts to check the progress of the enemy. Tomorrow morning, we will meet to discuss our plans, and you are welcome to join us." Aldren turned, and the overlords left the room.

Abbot Wilfrid had listened carefully throughout, "Thank you, Audric, and you, Tork, you have both put your lives at risk. I didn't like to mention it, but I have met Wulfhere twice in my time whilst spreading the word of God. As you say, he has a great religious belief, but I often wonder if he simply seeks to have God by his side in battle."

"We have two Christian kings about to wage war on each other, and I doubt any God would side with either of them," I replied.

Tork agreed, "I have been to battle in two wars and seen nothing but bloodshed. To cross the land after the fighting is over presents a sickening sight for all concerned."

"But we must defend our people and our land," countered the abbot.

"That will only be for the ones that survive. Many families will lose their menfolk," Tork answered.

I turned to Abbot Wilfrid and Tork, "There is no easy way through this. It will require the will of each kingdom to resolve a possible conflict, and at the moment, Wulfhere is intent on taking Northumbria by force. His father failed in his attempts, and this may be a sort of revenge in the eyes of Wulfhere. Let's see what Aldren has in mind tomorrow morning."

We left the abbot to his thoughts and walked despondently back to our shelter. Sleep was one way to seek refuge and avoid the real nightmare to come.

Our trek into Mercian territory had taken its toll, and we slept well and beyond our usual time of rising. The rain had stopped, and the quiet reminded me of the lull before a storm, but not the type we had just experienced. Tork was rubbing the sleep from his eyes, and on this occasion, looked a reluctant riser.

"Come on, Tork, we need to hear what our overlords have to say."

We dressed and went out into the open where the air was fresh, but there was mud everywhere, and the tree branches were drooping under the weight of rain droplets. Very few people were venturing out as we made our way up to the Northumbrian camp, where there was a lot of activity. Tents were being taken down, and it looked like those not already inside the walls were making ready to join those who had moved in whilst we were away. I felt that time was on our side, and the Mercians were unlikely to cross the river in Tadcaster for at least another two days. It might even take another day or two to move an entire army towards Eoforwic in the boggy conditions.

We saw Oldred commanding a group of men securing goods in a couple of carts and readying them for the horses nearby. He acknowledged our presence but made us wait a while before turning around and pointing to a nearby tent. We entered to find Aldren talking with four others who gave the appearance of other overlords or commanders. Their business finished, Aldren dismissed the group and they left while we remained, uncertain what to expect. We were beckoned to sit, and expectation was on all our faces, but no one rushed to speak. I went into a momentary trance, and the disturbing feeling experienced a few nights ago returned.

"You can't save Eoforwic. Leave and use your powers to lead Wulfhere and his mighty army to a great victory."

For a moment, I was locked in the grip of my alter ego and felt all-powerful until Tork intervened.

"Audric," he said and nudged me hard in the ribs.

Initially, I resented Tork's intervention and was about to curse him, but I quickly returned to reality. "Sorry," I offered, "my mind drifted off. Must have been a bad night." Once again, I felt unsettled and confused.

Oldred seemed unconcerned and was the first forthcoming. "That was one hell of a storm, and you're right; that should give us time to make preparations. As you see, we are moving the camp inside the walls, and we will use what is left of the Roman fort to barrack the men. We expect further armed men to arrive over the next two days. Scouts will go out today to see the progress made by the Mercians, and then I think we should launch a surprise attack rather than wait like lambs to the slaughter."

"And what are your thoughts, Aldren?" I asked as I attempted to recover my composure.

You could see by the way Aldren sat and positioned himself that he was in charge, but he carried a worried look and paused for a while before replying.

"Whilst we have lost and regained parts of Northumbria in the last decade, we are no longer the fighting force we used to be, and our numbers are well down, with many killed in battle. Wulfhere seems to have raised a strong army, and we need to bear that in mind. As Oldred suggests, a surprise attack may be our best option, but if our initial thrust fails, we will be wiped out. Our current position is our main strength, but we'll not be in a good position to feed ourselves indefinitely. But they will also suffer if holding us under siege. Their men will get weary and maybe lazy, possibly making them more vulnerable to a surprise attack at a later date. Perhaps most importantly, I don't want to lose more men unnecessarily. It has been a sad few years, and many friends have gone to their grave."

"I have never been to war," I replied, "and maybe I have no right to express my views, but I can see no value in war unless it is forced upon you. They have a numerical advantage, but it is not overwhelming, and we have the security of the walls and sufficient food and water for many months. However the battle develops, it seems likely that there will be large losses on both sides and little for the victors to celebrate. If you are determined to fight, I think we should retreat within the walls and look to defend our position. If they are repelled a few times and suffer losses, they may lose heart, and some of the recruits will probably abscond."

"You are full of words for one so young," argued Oldred. "We are warriors and born to fight. We have seen off the Mercians before and will do it again."

"No one doubts your bravery, Oldred," countered Aldren, "but you, yourself, have lost two brothers in battle, and I, many good friends. There is a time and place to fight. On this occasion, we may have no choice, but that doesn't mean throwing ourselves to the wolves. We will use brains rather than brawn and weigh our opportunity to strike back from within the walls. As for peace, we did not seek this battle, but nor will we flinch from our duty to protect Northumbria. Audric, you have shown courage in your efforts to help us, but you are released from further duty if you do not wish to fight for our cause."

"I will remain to protect the people of Northumbria, but my methods may differ from your own," I suggested. "I'm unlikely to ride into battle, but I will try to prevent the Mercians bringing tragedy to our door."

Aldren ordered, "Oldred, prepare our forces to defend Eoforwic but have them ready to attack outside the walls at short notice. I want guards stationed in all vulnerable positions and change them often to ensure they stay alert. As from tomorrow, we go on three-quarter rations. Keep the men in training but allow them plenty of rest. Send out fresh scouts each day, and they must be back before dark, or we go immediately into readiness for war. All the overlords will meet at dawn each day, and their second in command must check the guards each night. Meals are to be taken in rotation, so we are constantly prepared for an attack. We are not to be drawn into an offensive, however small their attacking numbers. They will tire in time and may take risks, and then we should take advantage. God speed us all."

Oldred left in a determined manner but didn't appear very pleased. We followed quickly behind when it was clear Aldren had finished with us all. I had an idea of how I might intervene in the battle, but I was still unsettled by my earlier experience.

"Tork, I hope this all works out. Let's have a drink and try to think of a less onerous matter."

Chapter 9

The next day everywhere was busy and armed men were moving around the town with great purpose. Orders were being snapped out, and men cursed beneath their breath.

"They seem to be organising well," said Tork. "It will be difficult for the Mercians to breach the walls, and the gates are very robust."

"I have been wondering if my powers might help, but they are not unlimited, and some only come to me on the spur of the moment, so I am never sure what interventions I may be able to use. For now, we will use our everyday efforts to protect ourselves and others. Though Aldren has sent out scouts, I think we will use Sher to track the enemy. Maybe we need to look at ways out if things go badly."

"It's good to hear you talk of some sort of escape, but why not go now?"

"It's a difficult balance, Tork. I feel an obligation to the abbot and the local settlers here and throughout Northumbria. If Wulfhere rides roughshod through Eoforwic, then he will continue north. Remember the friends we have made on our journey so far. I have less concern for Aldren and his men as they have chosen this way of life, but their efforts will be needed to defeat the Mercians. On this occasion, it will be more about saving as many lives as possible."

"Then I'll get on with my task and see you mid-afternoon near the library."

I walked through one of the main gates and felt a sense of foreboding as if the battle was imminent. I summoned Sher and watched the skyline, and on this occasion, he swooped in low from the nearby woodland and landed on my extended arm, already looking back the way as if knowing the task ahead. I drew a few images in the loose soil and pointed back through the woodland. Sher raised his wings, and I felt his power as he pushed off and soared into the distance.

I later caught up with Tork near the steps to the library, and we walked on whilst he told me how he'd fared.

"I've found a route out on the northern wall. We'll need a rope to lower ourselves to the ground, and then there's cover as we dash to nearby woodland."

"Hopefully, we won't need it," I replied and explained that Sher had been sent to search out the Mercians and would be back soon.

Tension was building, and Aldren's men were looking well prepared, but a sense of fear also pervaded the crowds as they moved around. It would probably be another two days before the main attacking forces could reach us, but it was reassuring to see us well prepared. We returned to our quarters and checked our horses were fed and watered, then ate outside whilst checking our weapons.

Suddenly I heard a flurry of flapping wings, and Sher appeared out of the blue, alert as ever and sat on the ground nearby. He strutted around in that familiar way of his as if every movement meant something. This went on for some length of time, and we were enjoying the spectacle when Sher stopped, gave his usual squawk and flew off. Tork looked at me expectantly as I rose from the ground with a worried look on my face.

"Well, Tork, they are on their way and making progress, but as expected, the main group are moving slowly and are bogged down in parts, finding it difficult to keep the overloaded carts on the go. But of more concern is a group of horsemen, probably two hundred, riding quickly, coming in from the east. They could make a surprise attack if they don't realise we are well prepared. Aldren's scouts are nearing the enemy lines but have missed the flanking movement. My guess is that they think Eoforwic is poorly protected and that our army is still further north, in and around Aldren's estates in Durham. They have hopes to ride straight through the main gate and secure the town."

"Then they're in for a big surprise," Tork said cheerily, "though they will quickly spot the guards and the security on the gates."

"Maybe; we need to see Aldren as soon as possible."

We hurried our way to Aldren's new quarters; everyone now barracked inside the remains of the old Roman fort and made our presence known to his guards. Oldred appeared wearing his usual, stern face and led us back into the shelter where Aldren sat in discussion with another overlord we'd seen before.

Aldren put us under one of his stares. "You have some news even before we have our own scouts back for the day. I hope this is no trickery. I have trusted you so far, but I would hate to be ambushed in my own camp."

"I perform no trickery," I retorted, but paused as I thought about how to explain our new information. Even if they accepted I had certain powers, I doubted they would believe I used a bird to track and detail the position of the enemy. "Tork went out at night and used his well-honed tracking skills."

"So, what did he find out?" asked Aldren.

"As hoped for, after the storm, the main body of the Mercians are bogged down and will not reach us in less than two days, but we have discovered they have sent about two hundred well-armed men, all on horseback, on ahead. That number suggests they intend some form of attack and don't know that Eoforwic is so strongly defended. They will ride straight through the gate, if they can, to try and secure the town ready for the rest of the army. If there was any stronger resistance, they would expect walls to be manned and the gates closed and then they would back off ready to lay siege."

"So, what do you suggest?" challenged Oldred.

"Put the Mercians in a position where they have a difficult choice to make. What do they value most, more land or the lives of their men who are friends or have a desire to survive? We may have an opportunity to reduce their attacking numbers and use those captured to work out a peaceful solution for the long term. Having met Wulfhere, I feel he is someone who will listen to reason, but we can't be sure until we have the chance to negotiate with him. I outlined a plan of action. Remember this could save many Northumbrian lives both now and in the future, including your own, Oldred."

The idea of his own death seemed to calm Oldred, and nearby, Aldren sat in thought.

"Once again, you have spoken wisely, and we have nothing to lose if we're careful. But, if the Mercians fall into our trap and don't surrender quickly, they will be slaughtered without hesitation. From what you say, we need to be ready by early morning as they may send out scouts of their own before riding into Eoforwic."

We drifted out of the shelter and walked on to our dwelling room. Oldred had agreed to meet us there later and bring along some of the overlords.

"Do you think Oldred can be trusted?" asked Tork.

"Not entirely, but we have no choice; this is not our war. Oldred doesn't like to take advice from someone as young as me. Aldren is much more careful and ready to listen to reason. He seems to hold the respect of his men, so if we plan well, then hopefully, there will be no carnage."

Our meeting with Oldred and the other overlords went well, and they seemed content to be readying for battle after days on end of relative inactivity. That evening the preparations were completed to give the appearance of normality. The guards were doubled for the night, but only a few observers kept a lookout. Archers slept in the positions they had been shown, and armed men were nearby to provide backup. About fifty horses were tethered, ready for use if the Mercians broke through.

Tork and I slept fitfully on the wall near the main gate. Oldred was a short distance away, but there had been little conversation since the men had settled. I woke often and wished something would happen, but Tork seemed fast asleep. Small groups of men were sitting around talking in whispers adding even more tension to the atmosphere.

The sun would rise soon, but there was no sight nor sound of the enemy. Most of the men were now awake, chewing on bits of food and checking their weapons. My stomach began to churn as I thought of two hundred armed riders, probably their elite warriors, readying to take Eoforwic by force. Tork moved, then woke with a start, looking up to see Sher on my hand before he flew off.

"Their men are on the move, Tork, and should be seen shortly."

"I'll tell Oldred to prepare," said Tork, "and then we can move to the main gate."

It seemed a long while before we heard the noise of hooves drumming away and dust rising in the distance. The warriors paused about half a mile away, then a group of five came forward and rode slowly towards the gate, stopping about two-thirds of the way there. They could see the gate was open, and there was no activity so early in the morning. There were no men on the gate or the walls. They edged forward a bit further, paused again, before turning and riding back to the group. A rider came to the front, raised a large flag and then rode forward. He was followed a short distance behind by the Mercians in random formation, looking every bit ready for battle. There was no screaming or shouting, just the increasing noise of the horses picking up their pace. All our men were hidden, and no one was trying to watch their approach. It was all down to them entering the snare.

Whilst the horses came at a canter, what happened next seemed to take place at walking pace. First, the flag bearer rode majestically into view through the gate and took everyone's attention; several lead riders appeared, followed by a slow parade of others until more than half of the enemy were within the gate. Then the trance was broken as a net was dropped into place, bringing the parade of riders to a sudden halt. The gate was closed, and shouting came from everywhere. The front riders realised their way forward was blocked. They turned to look for a way out but soon ran up against their fellow riders, so they bunched together, almost in a circle. They could see the trap quite clearly now with archers all around ready to fire their arrows and many men ready with lethal spears. They scurried about in panic, waiting for their leader to give the word, but nothing came.

A couple of riders made for what they thought might be a way through but were struck down by several arrows. Their leader grabbed the flag, threw it to the ground and slowly dismounted. He unbuckled his belt, and his sword fell to the ground. He had assessed the situation very quickly. With no barrage of arrows or spears beyond the first shots, he knew the Northumbrians were looking for them to surrender. Anything else would see them all dead in a very short time. There was screaming and shouting from outside the walls as men were trying to save the situation but were being cut down as they attempted to scale the parapets.

Back inside, one by one, the Mercians accepted their fate and followed the example of their leader, but staying close to their weapons, suspicious that they may yet be attacked. When the stand-off seemed settled, Aldren appeared on his large white stead. He edged slowly towards the Mercians and raised his arm. The archers lowered their bows but remained at the ready.

"There will be no more fighting within these walls if you surrender, and your lives will be spared if your king agrees to withdraw from Northumbria. We have no wish for war, but you can already see we are well prepared, even for the mighty Wulfhere. If your leader says yes, then you will be restrained under armed guard and held in small groups until we have spoken to your king. You will receive food and water, but if anyone in your group tries to break free, we will kill all in that group. Could your leader come forward to speak?"

A huge man, the one who had thrown the flag to the ground, walked forward. He hit his arm on his chest in a gesture of acceptance and a final degree of defiance. "We accept your offer, but I'm not sure you will have such luck with the king."

"Then you will die before you have time to fight again," explained Aldren. I understand Wulfhere is a man of reason, so pray that he is, and we can all go back to our homelands in peace. Your men have retreated on the other side of the wall to a safe distance. Send one of your men over the wall with a message that you are all safe for now but that Aldren calls for a meeting with Wulfhere to discuss terms."

A man was despatched with a look of relief on his face. He was lowered over the wall and ran to the remainder of the Mercians, passing several bodies on the way. He spoke for a short while and was then heaved onto the back of one of the horses, and they rode off at a great pace.

I had watched all this with great relief. Not one Northumbrian had been killed, but I had to remind myself that over two thousand armed men were still out there ready to cut our throats. Maybe they will listen to reason, but if not, they will fight with real anger after our small victory.

I walked over to Tork and suggested, "Keep a watchful eye on where the Mercians are tied up, particularly their leader. He must not come to any harm. Praise Oldred for his efforts; we need to keep him on our side. I'm going to see the abbot; he could be a key figure in all this."

"The first part of the plan has gone well," Tork proffered. "I'll see you later."

Tork drifted around as the Mercians were split into several groups, and their hands and feet were bound. They were moved to individual compounds and left under guard. Their leader stood out with his great height, and they all looked resigned to the situation but glad to be alive.

Oldred walked my way and approached with a smile on his face. "I never imagined facing Mercian fighters and not running them through with my sword, but I must admit to enjoying our success today. Let's hope the plan continues in the same vein, or we're in for a long confrontation."

"Aye, you've done well, and your men were disciplined in bringing the enemy to heel. Remember, these men are very important in our bargaining power and mustn't be harmed."

"Your friend is starting to win me over, but he's no older than my son and I couldn't imagine taking orders from him."

Tork replied, "Don't think of his words as orders, just advice that you would have thought of sooner or later."

"Shall we get a drink?" said Oldred. "I have a mighty thirst."

I was still looking for the abbot when I observed Tork and Oldred in the distance enjoying a drink and laughing as if all our problems were solved. I smiled and thought they should enjoy the moment.

Chapter 10

Another dawn arrived, and it was no surprise to see Tork outside, taking in the cool morning air. He had already been down to where the Mercians were being held, and all looked in order. Many were still sleeping whilst others wriggled around to relieve the aches and pains in their bodies. I contemplated how we would release these men and not have them return to do their worst. It would be impossible to retain them too long as eventually, they would become a danger within our camp.

"Morning," Tork said, "I have looked in on the Mercians, and they are all fine, if a little sore after a night tied up."

"Thanks, Tork. I went down there last night with Abbot Wilfrid, and he confirmed what I was thinking - that their leader is Wulfhere's brother, AEhtelred. He is taller than Wulfhere, but their facial features are very alike. Hopefully, that will help our negotiations with their king. Let's go and eat; I can't see the enemy reaching Eoforwic until midday. Then we need to take the abbot to see Aldren and Oldred."

By the time we were fed, the sun was up, and the early mist was lifting when we entered Aldren's tent. Oldred was there and gave us a friendly nod and smile.

Aldren turned to see we had Abbot Wilfrid alongside us, "Hello, Abbot Wilfrid, what brings you here so early?"

"Audric feels that I can be of use in dealing with Wulfhere; I'll let him explain."

"The abbot has confirmed that the leader of the captives is Wulfhere's brother."

"Is he indeed," interrupted Aldren.

"Abbot Wilfrid has met both brothers twice on his religious travels and says they are confirmed Christians. He believes Wulfhere will do anything to rescue his brother and will have a great desire not to lose some of the elite men. If Wulfhere accepts your offer of a meeting, I think you should take Abbot Wilfrid with you. First and foremost, they must withdraw their men back into Mercia. As a concession, you can agree to release fifteen men, but AEthelred, Wulfhere's brother, should not be released yet. Wulfhere should be asked to swear to God in the abbot's presence that he will not return to Northumbria during the remainder of his life. When your scouts confirm the Mercians are back in Mercia, the remaining men will be released without arms. AEthelred will also be asked to swear to stay out of Northumbria until his brother's death."

"Can we trust their word?" said Aldren. "Men who were about to purge our kingdom and slit our throats?"

"I believe they are God-fearing men," I answered, "and will not take their oaths lightly. One of the reasons they take to the faith is their belief in the power of God, who is all-seeing and all-hearing. You have also defeated them in a strategic way, and Wulfhere will be wary of returning anytime soon. In such circumstances, you are no worse off, as long as you maintain your guard."

Aldren looked around at everyone and saw no further words forthcoming. "If this comes off, you will deserve your own land or some reward."

"To be clear," I replied, "I seek no reward other than to save the lives of hundreds of people."

"I can't guarantee that," said Aldren, "though your plan has a good chance of success. But first, we must hear from Wulfhere.

Remember, his intention was war, and even the possible loss of his brother may not hold him back."

"We should see them soon enough," I suggested, "maybe after midday. As you say, they may attack straight away, so we need to be prepared."

We left the abbot with Aldren to have further discussions and headed back to our dwelling.

I started to think of the meeting of the two leaders when Tork questioned, "Is there a risk the Mercians might try to take Aldren captive?"

"Maybe, but the leaders can look after themselves, and both will be cautious. The risk is worth taking."

We sat and talked about what we might do if the kingdoms decided on peace. I suggested that I was ready to move on and wanted nothing more to do with the warring factions. Tork said he was relieved to hear that, as his mind and body no longer had a taste for fighting. I still desired to see new places and more cultural and peaceful activities.

By late afternoon, there was a great expectation inside the walls. The men in the barrack area were tense, expecting an attack despite holding the captives. Then the silence was broken by the rumbling of horses that could be heard in the distance, gradually getting louder and louder. Soon, out towards the Fosse Way, the Mercian army unfolded, lining up in the distance to show its strength. The armed men banged their spears on their shields and then shouted insults and threats that were lost in the wind. It would not have taken much to rouse these men to attack, but as fast as they had arrived, most of the army turned and disappeared out of view.

A small group remained of about twenty men, all mounted. At their head was someone who looked like Wulfhere. They rode a little closer, and then one rider broke from the group and moved slowly towards the gate. This was the Mercian sent back to deliver a message about the captives and Wulfhere's brother. He stuck his spear in the ground, continued to the gate and waited at the base of the wall. A rope was thrown down, and the man was hauled up onto the rampart. He was taken to Aldren, and, after talking for a good while, the man returned the way he had come. We stayed out of view and watched events unfold.

Aldren, Abbot Wilfrid and twenty armed men on horseback left their secure position as the gates were opened and quickly shut again. They rode to stop a short distance from the Mercian group, and then Aldren stuck his spear in the ground and passed his shield to another rider. He and Abbot Wilfrid rode halfway closer to the Mercians and waited. Wulfhere and an unarmed guard made their way to meet them. They all dismounted and sat down. The talking went on for some time until they rose as the sun was going down.

Aldren and the abbot returned, and there was a great sense of relief as they came through the gate safely; but what sort of message had they brought back?

Aldren moved to the library steps and was soon surrounded by many of his men. He paused until there was a degree of quiet and then began.

"Mighty Northumbrians, you have won the day, and the Mercians will withdraw tomorrow."

There was an almighty roar and noise from the crashing of shields; then, Aldren raised his arm to silence them.

"They will retreat to their kingdom and have vowed not to invade again in the lifetime of Wulfhere, provided we do the same. Both sides have sworn to peace by almighty God and will be subject to his wrath if either kingdom goes against the words of their king."

There were more excited rumblings, and some men even hugged their nearest friend. Aldren allowed them their moment of relief and looked around the crowd. The message was getting to the men still guarding the walls, and cheers began to echo all around. He raised an arm again, and the men held back their elation to hear more.

"We must stay alert until we are sure the Mercians have fully withdrawn. Some of the Mercian hostages will be released in the morning, and a few of our men will follow their retreat south. Only once our men confirm they have left Northumbria will we allow the remaining captives to go free. Understand that no harm must come to the captives, or peace may be lost. So, take heed, there must be no celebrations until we are sure we have rid them from our kingdom."

"Long live the king!" shouted Oldred, and the words echoed around the crowd. Gradually the men dispersed, and we saw the opportunity to go over to Aldren and Abbot Wilfrid.

Aldren saw us approaching and moved past his men. "Well, young man, we have a lot to thank you for. I fear we were hell-bound for war until you brought us back to our senses. You must join our forces, and I'll reward you with some title."

I paused, then replied, "You are very generous, and everyone is proud when their efforts receive such recognition. I could not ask for more, but my ambitions lie elsewhere, and if I achieve success, I will return to enjoy your hospitality."

"I guessed you might say that," retorted Aldren. "You are far from an ordinary young man, but I wish you all the best. Stay until we have our celebrations, and we can drink to your good health."

"That would be very welcome in normal times, but if Wulfhere breaks his word, there will be an unimaginable carnage, and I don't want to be involved. We'll risk a lonely journey through their lands and take our chances that way. They have no knowledge of our involvement in this standoff, so it is better we move away as soon as possible."

Tork nodded his agreement, and we shook the hands of Aldren and Oldred, then walked away with their best wishes.

"Thank you, Tork," I said. "I'm glad that you are prepared to continue our journey. I'd be lost without you."

"Aye, you would that, but one of these days, we must stay for the celebration and to hell with the enemy."

"Hopefully, we will have many more times to celebrate. Let's catch up with the abbot before we go. I sense this is not the last time we will see him."

It was now dark, and only the moonlight and a few torches lit our way to his dwelling. His assistant took us through to the abbot's room, and he greeted us with a worn expression on his face. Clearly, the meeting with Wulfhere had taken its toll. I explained that we had come to say goodbye and we would leave in the morning.

Abbot Wilfrid smiled gently. "You have made a good decision; this is no life for a young man like you, but I will be sorry to see you depart. There is still a lot of work to be done back at the abbey if you return to Hexham, though I sense you have a need to move on."

"We'll go south, Abbot, but one day I hope to return and see the new abbey in all its magnificence. Take care, Abbot Wilfrid - not all our countrymen have Christian virtues. Your land and buildings could come under attack. Stay close to Aldren and Wulfhere for the moment whilst they are at peace."

"Once again, thank you for your advice. Have a good journey, and may God be with you both."

I lay back in my bunk that night and gradually slipped into a deep sleep, contemplating our efforts over the last few days, but I might have anticipated I would not be allowed to wallow in our success.

"You turned down the offer of land and title from Aldren. Are you mad?"

"*Those are not the things I seek.*"

"*Are you not perhaps deceiving yourself? Will you live as a peasant the rest of your life?*"

"*No, but there are other ways to prosper.*"

"*I believe you are ambitious?*"

"*Yes, but…*"

"*I know, it's not the same! You think you succeeded today, but it's a false dawn.*"

"*What do you mean? We saved many lives.*"

"*You only delayed the inevitable. The Mercians are livid, and someone will suffer their wrath soon enough.*"

"*They have sworn to God not to attack each other.*"

"*You are very naïve young Audric; remember, I share your powers. There will be war again soon and widespread carnage.*"

"*I cannot be everywhere at once.*"

"*That's right; you should go your own way and look after your own interests.*"

"*Let's see what the future holds. Take yourself away!*"

"*Indeed, indeed!*"

It seemed a long night, and many thoughts rattled through my mind.

By dawn, I was awake and feeling that my head had taken a battering. "Not again!" I screamed.

Tork wandered into my room. "Have you had a nightmare?" he asked. "You were talking in your sleep again, though much seemed nonsense."

"That's what it is, nonsense. Give me a short while to collect my thoughts, and we'll go and enjoy the cool morning air."

The sharp breeze restored my senses, but I was still unsettled. "Tork, do you think I should have accepted Aldren's offer of land and title?"

"Aye, well, it seemed tempting at the time. Why? Do you doubt your decision now? I'm sure he would still honour his pledge."

"Was I right to interfere in their battle? Won't they just be at each other's throats in the future?"

"Your cage seems to have been rattled. Do you doubt yourself now? Your decisions and the outcomes seem good to me."

"Maybe, I need to settle myself. Some of Morgan's influences may also have stimulated disturbing thoughts. Only time will tell."

"Your instincts have been well-judged. Trust them. Once a decision has been made, doubt has no place to interfere."

"Thanks, Tork. Let's get ready to journey on."

We were both alert and had organised our packs by the time the early morning mist started to lift with a good day in prospect. I chose to dress in my monk's robe as there was every possibility that we might meet stray Mercian warriors. Our plan was to make for a settlement called Lundenwic on the edge of the old Roman town of Londinium, now largely unused, according to Abbot Wilfrid. The land had been absorbed into the Mercian kingdom in recent years, though the former king was allowed to continue to act as overlord to the former Kingdom of Essex. Lundenwic was growing rapidly following the repeated invasions, mainly by Saxons, and it was becoming a busy trading town for goods coming in from the rest of the world. It was one further step in my desire to see more and learn how the trading world worked as it seemed to reflect a much wider cultural society than existed in most of Britain.

Part 2

A Brighter Future

Chapter 11

Our journey south was largely uneventful on our long trek, mainly following the old Roman roads, and I sensed Audric was now settled after the events in Eoforwic. We saw nothing of Wulfhere's men but did ponder if they had stuck to their word. We stayed over at several farm settlements where the reception was friendly and camped nearby. By now, Audric had returned to wearing his normal clothes and was no longer the travelling monk.

Most of the time, the roads were quiet, but occasionally, families were passing by looking for new pastures to improve their lives. We also met a few traders moving their goods by horse and cart. Audric showed his interest but bought nothing, despite his enthusiasm for the goods on offer. There was talk of goods from Eurasia, the Byzantine, Syria and as far afield as China; all lands we had only heard about in our very limited travels and stories passed down the generations. There were tales of treasure and extravagant items discovered in burial sites and dug up on farmland. These were largely left by the Romans when they returned home and laid undiscovered for centuries until some lucky person disturbed the hiding places.

"Tork, do you not wonder what sorts of societies exist in the world to create this degree of extravagance?" asked Audric.

I looked at the beautiful jewellery nearby, "I do think why we in Britain are so poor that such items are way beyond our dreams," I answered.

"It's not just that. Think of the skill involved and how the goods reflect far more advanced civilisations. I have a great desire to see such cultural development. I may have inherited powers to do good, but they must be embedded in the real world to be meaningful."

"Then there should be interesting times ahead."

After three weeks on the road, we started to see old stone markers showing we were closing in on our final destination. We were beginning to come across villages that appeared well established with dwellings and huts of more substantial construction and size. Some had small but prominent churches though not of the scale being built back in Hexham and Ripon. Occasionally, bands of armed men were evident, looking busy heading this way and that, suggesting nobility ruled the lands nearby.

Looking into the distance, we could now see the old Roman walls of Londinium, and they dominated the view, making us all the more surprised that the land inside was no longer occupied. We knew we had to get closer to the northern walls then turn to the west to pick out Lundenwic, again following a Roman road and other well-worn tracks running alongside.

We were then entering Lundenwic, which was full of activity and more people than I'd seen in years.

"It's a little overwhelming with all these crowds," I commented.

"I understand your concern, but we're not far from open land and the forests we passed earlier. The place is full of life, and I think it will provide us with many opportunities when we understand how the town thrives."

"Maybe, but you might lose the robe on your back if you don't sleep with one eye open around here."

"You could be right, Tork. We'll need to be worldly-wise as we get to understand the dangers, but I hope we will gain more than we lose. Whilst we may make wealth, that will only be a measure of the progress made in learning more about how the world and society can develop. Let's see if we can find bunks for the night, and tomorrow we will begin to explore the town."

"Anything must be better than waiting for Mercian armed men coming to draw blood."

"Let your mind move on and look to a rosy future. Maybe a drink will relax you."

"Aye, we'll raise a jug to the celebrations we left behind in Eoforwic."

We rarely drank in this fashion, but that evening we found joy in a few drinks, reflecting on the past few years and what we might look out for tomorrow. Audric's plan was becoming a little clearer, but as always, his ideas seemed to carry a degree of risk.

In the morning, we dressed in our best clothes, which, to be honest, were those from the previous day with small adornments, and tied back our hair after a good wash. Audric secured his coinage, and I slipped a knife into my bootlegging when I thought he wasn't looking.

"Let's hope we don't need that," said Audric, smiling.

"Aye, well, if I have to use it, I hope my enemy is not as smart as you."

"Your protection is very welcome; just be careful. I would rather lose my coinage than a good friend."

Today we would trail around town and understand the layout. Our room for the night was part of someone's home, and drinks had been served on tables and benches outside in the street. There were a few similar places nearby, and the nightlife had been rowdy late into the darkness. As we progressed, we started to see open-fronted dwellings selling simple bits and pieces; mainly pottery, firewood and stiff brushes for the home. Then we came upon a square with many stalls tightly packed selling a wide range of farm produce, including slaughtered pigs hung from spikes in tripod formation.

Some stalls had heavy blades for butchering the animals. As in Hexham, some meat was being cooked on spits and being eaten in the street, mainly by young men showing a degree of wealth in their clothing and through a display of coins in payment.

Audric's eyes were elsewhere, drawn to a row of stalls with foreign goods on display. One immediately drew my attention with large furs in shades and tones of black and brown, almost certainly bearskins. Nearby were different types of animal tusks in a range of sizes. Then there were remarkable carvings made from the tusks, which demonstrated incredible artistic ability and imagination. Audric was very interested in the silver dishes and the beautifully embossed work that made them stand out. The pottery was of great quality and embellished in many designs that caught the eye. Wonderful necklaces were hanging there made from ornate beads and beautifully coloured glass. Embroidered silk robes and garments seemed fit for a king or queen, yet there were many on show of varying size and colour.

Audric shouted to one of the stallholders, "How do you sell such wonderful items to people of little means?"

The man on the stall pondered Audric. "With great difficulty, but the local nobility know we set up here in the market and, every now and then, they visit to make a purchase. We need to come every market day or risk missing their visits. They come long distances as there is nowhere else you can buy such wonderful and original pieces. On occasions, we're asked to visit them to display new goods. Apart from the nobility, there're a few rich merchants in the town who've made their wealth through trading who seek our goods for themselves or to sell on. Now m' lad, have you enough coinage in that bag tied to your waist to buy something, or have I been wasting my time talking to you?"

We laughed, and Audric replied, "I think it's about time I tried to buy something, but how do I know what it might be worth?"

The trader laughed in response. "Now you want all my secrets. That's what we call the risk you take. Just imagine buying cattle; the more you have worked on farmland, the more likely you understand the quality of the animals. As far as my jewellery is concerned, if you intend it for yourself or a loved one, it doesn't really matter if you have the wealth, but if you hope to sell it on, then that's your dilemma. Now, can I sell you a silver ring?"

"I'll give you three shillings for that ring there."

"Now you've got the idea, but no, I want six shillings. It's very well crafted, as you have noticed."

"I'll let you have four shillings, my best offer."

"Five, and it's yours."

"Sorry, four is my last offer. I'm sure you would like to go home with coins in your own bag."

The man held out his hand, "You learn quickly, m'lad, but take care as it takes time to learn the trade, and there are some real crooks out there ready to swindle you. I might be one of them."

Audric took the ring and placed it on a finger of his right hand and admired it. "Two more questions if I may?"

"If you keep buying, you can ask as many questions as you like."

"Where did it come from?"

"That probably comes from the Rhineland where silver can be mined, and there're skilled craftsmen who work together in an emporium. I buy from merchants who come off boats from overseas, and the goods could be sold two or three times before reaching Britain."

What's an emporium?"

"It's like a settlement or small area within a town where special goods are made by skilled men and women. They are then sold to merchants who trade locally or travel overseas to buy more goods or exchange or sell what they have bought from the emporium."

"What about people who have little or no coinage? How do they manage to buy such goods?"

"Most of the time they can't, but individuals and people in collectives can trade their own goods; silver from Cornwall, pottery from Gippeswic in East Anglia and farmers can offer their live sheep, plus sheep's wool and cattle hides in exchange. Here in Lundenwic, the emporium is growing. Small workshops are opening, and they're manned by craftsmen who've travelled to Britain to start a new life, possibly because of persecution in their homeland. Most of the really exotic goods are from overseas, and more are reaching Briton each year. Being a merchant's not an easy life. They are often despised because of their apparent wealth, and envy can attract violence."

"How do you become a merchant?" I queried.

"Your friend seems too young to be a merchant but talks like someone many years older. First, find people who you can trust who're in the trade, then build up your knowledge step by step. Specialise in one part and keep your trading small until your confidence grows. I can't afford to use you, but you can ask for my advice and repay me if you are successful. My name is Franco, and you can find me here most market days."

"It all seems overwhelming at the moment, but there is great interest there for me. My name is Audric, and this is my friend, Tork. We look forward to seeing you again soon. Thank you for the ring."

"Just to be clear, it's me that thanks you. Have good fortune, Audric."

We wandered off and Audric glanced at his new ring. I wondered what was on Audric's mind. "That's a fine piece of jewellery, but it won't feed or clothes us every day," I jested.

"Sorry, Tork, I should have discussed the ring with you before buying, but I promise you'll get your share soon enough."

"Share a ring? Now you have me confused."

"Allow me a little time, and let's see what else we can discover about this place."

"Aye, it's fascinating. Let's see if we can find one of the workshops Franco mentioned."

"Just what I was thinking."

As the morning progressed, we saw many dwellings closely packed and what looked like workshops scattered here and there.

I was glancing back as I sauntered on some distance ahead of Audric when he shouted, "Look out, Tork!"

I felt my legs knocked from beneath me and went tumbling headfirst to the ground. I heard laughter and looked side on from my prone position. I saw two young men, one holding a staff in his hand, the reason for my downfall. I lay a few moments longer to size up my situation and noticed Audric leaning on a post, nodding to me that the lads had tripped me.

As I rose, the youngsters laughed again, and one shouted, "At least you didn't have to fall far."

"Aye, well, that may be true, but it wasn't a kind thing to do."

I had my knife strapped to the side of my boot, but didn't want to make this altercation too serious, so I removed the knife and threw it with pinpoint accuracy into a narrow tree trunk well away from harm.

"So, which one of you would like to try that again?" I asked with measured determination.

The young men turned more serious and started to circle me, both now carrying staffs in a menacing fashion. Audric still hadn't moved but was watching intently.

Suddenly he edged away from the post, shouting, "Here, Tork, catch."

I barely saw what was coming until it landed in my hand from at least thirty strides away. So it was to be my fight with a useful looking staff. The lads stepped back at first, then continued to circle, obviously still fancying their chances.

"So, it's a fair fight now? A dwarf against two strapping young men," I challenged.

One made a stabbing thrust with his staff which I deflected and then wrapped him hard on the knuckles. The other came from the side, but I reversed my staff hard into his groin, causing him to double up. Then a blow to the back of his neck sent him groaning to the ground. The one still standing lurched forward, attempting a massive blow to my head, and I moved slightly to the side and placed my staff between his arms before wrenching his weapon from his hands. Two more thrusts to his chest and a gentle shove sent him sprawling in a pile over his friend's dormant body.

I noticed Sher overhead. Too late, I thought, but he swooped to the ground and began pecking away at the two bodies as if he was a vulture about to eat its prey. A crowd had developed, and there was a sudden outburst of laughter and cheers.

Audric walked across. "If I'd known it was going to take you so long, I might have joined in!"

I smiled, "Thanks for the staff and not intervening. It's some time since I had a good scrap."

"Sher, away," shouted Audric.

We watched him stare into the eyes of one of the combatants as if to warn against further trouble, and then he flew away majestically into the distant skyline.

The crowd began to disperse, and the two young men recovered their senses and made a hasty retreat. Despite the excitement, we decided to continue with our exploring of the town. We chose a large workshop and went to the entrance to look in. At benches, four women were working on finished hides, cutting them into sections. Nearby, workmen were moulding, stretching and stitching the leather into boots with wooden soles.

"They look grand," I said. "I could do with a new pair of boots. These are well worn."

Audric smiled, "Then you shall have a pair, my good friend."

"Nah, too expensive for boots that good. I'm no prince yet."

"I have an idea. Let me do the talking."

"When did I never?"

Audric called out, "Can we talk with someone about your boots?"

One of the women stood up from her workbench. "How can we help you?" She had a pleasant smile, and Audric smiled back.

"Could you make a fine pair of boots for each of us?"

"They will take two days to make, and you have to pay one silver shilling upfront for each pair and a further two shillings for each pair on collection: six shillings in all. Have you got that much coinage? Sorry to be so blunt, but we work long hours and need to be rewarded."

"We don't have any coinage," lied Audric, "but we do have a high-value silver ring of great craftsmanship."

"That would be a first," she replied. "Our master is the only one who could agree that; wait here."

When she reappeared from out the back, she was joined by a well-built middle-aged man of youthful appearance. "My wife says you would like to pay for some new boots by trading a silver ring," queried the man.

Audric took the ring off his finger and passed it to the man. "Try it on."

The ring slipped neatly over the man's knuckle, and he stood there admiring it. "I can see it's finely crafted, and the silver weight seems right. What do you want for the ring?"

"It's worth at least eight shillings, or the two pairs of boots plus two shillings in return."

"I don't doubt its real value, but the best I can do is take the ring for all the work on the boots. I'll ensure they are the best boots you've ever worn."

"Well, the boots are more important to us at the moment, so we accept your offer." Audric shook the man's hand but asked if he could keep the ring until the boots were made.

"You seem trustworthy, sit over there whilst I take some measurements." The cobbler pulled out some pieces of string and measured our feet and calves, tying knots here and there. "Where are you from?"

"Just down from Eoforwic," replied Audric.

"We hear there was trouble up that way."

"Yes, we heard the same thing. All was settled, we understand, without too much fighting."

"They're lucky. Wulfhere has taken over some of the kingdoms down this way. There was little fighting as the overlords just gave in. In return, the overlords have been left in place, subject to the loss of certain bits of land and a commitment to support his army when needed."

"Sounds like it might be for the best," concluded Audric.

"Whilst I can carry on working in peace, I'm happy enough, but I don't want my sons taken off to war. Come back tomorrow evening just before sundown. The boots might need some final adjustments, but we'll see."

We walked out, and I said, "Your first trade and what a fine deal that was."

"Maybe I will take a liking to this way of life," replied Audric.

"Well, if it keeps me in boots, I won't complain."

We spent the rest of the day visiting other workshops, some just sole traders and others with up to twenty people working in two or three buildings. As suggested by Franco, several traders were foreigners who had brought their skills and goods to Britain when faced with difficult times in their homeland. There were pottery and glass manufacturers from the Rhineland and Scandinavia. From Italy and Spain, there were makers of fine silver items of all types, from adornments to bowls and chalices. Women at one workshop had thousands of colourful glass beads brought with them from Central Asia, which they threaded onto fine cord to make beautiful bracelets and necklaces. We heard stories of trade routes across deserts and mountains from places like Byzantium and China. The traders showed us exotic garments and rolls of fine silk that they sell to rich nobility and landowners. We contrasted the thin, smooth silk against our own robes made of rough wool and linen. Despite the silk's fine thread, it was very strong and belied its beautiful texture.

Some traders were just dealers selling stocks of oils, spices and wines. They explained how some had medicinal potency and others could enrich food when cooking. Audric asked many questions and the traders were very friendly and helpful, happy to talk about their wonderfully crafted goods.

The following day, we wandered a little further from the centre. We found three buildings used for the manufacture of pottery with unique designs and not your typical earthenware used in most dwellings. The trader had come from Italy a few years ago and sold their goods to the better-off Britons and to merchants who travelled to different countries. We returned to our dwelling and then walked to the riverbank, where we found more surprises. Whilst we had seen occasional small boats on our travels, now we were seeing large numbers of all shapes and sizes, probably reflecting the styles of their homelands.

Timber crates were being hauled on and off the boats, and horses and carts were nearby to move the goods inland. Pulleys and decks were in use, similar to those used in constructing the abbeys we had helped build. Noise came from all around as men shouted at their crew, and they responded in kind. The scene was one of constant activity – as if every moment mattered. Here and there, we spotted well-dressed men who we took to be the merchants watching the workers and passing advice to their gang leaders. This was our first evidence of how widespread trading was taking place in and beyond Britain.

Looking at some of the boats, we wondered how they safely moved the goods across the oceans and the risks the crews took in handling the boats. I had stood on the seashore a few times with my former master and seen the violence of the waves when the storms occurred, but we never travelled out to sea.

"These boats are not for me," I shouted over the rabble of noise.

"They also strike me with a degree of fear, but they are the only way to explore beyond these shores," responded Audric. "Don't worry; we have lots to do before we can consider travelling to other lands."

"It seems a lot of risk, just to move exotic goods back and forth."

"I'm sure the rewards are great, and the adventure must attract many to make these difficult journeys. One day I want to explore these far-off lands, but first, there is much we can learn on these shores. Let's go get those boots."

"Feet on dry land will keep me happy."

The master cobbler was at the entrance to his works taking a break and raised his hand when we came in view.

"Fine day. Take a seat inside; I'll be with you shortly. The boots are ready if you have the ring."

A short while later, we pulled on the boots and walked back and forth to try them out.

"Mine feel great," said Audric.

"Same here," I agreed.

"If you get a bit of tightness around the toes, they will stretch in time. Come back if you need any alteration. We can make you a fine jacket to go with the boots."

"Thanks for the boots, but the jackets will have to wait."

We left the cobbler, Arrandi, admiring the ring whilst we paraded along in the new boots back to our dwelling, contemplating our first trade.

"Well, Tork, how do we progress to become master traders with relatively little coinage or goods to exchange?"

"I thought you were the brains in this adventure. Farming and building are all we've ever done, and that required long hours just to keep a roof over our heads. Master used to make potions and oils for ailments but seemed to give them away most of the time."

"Maybe I can combine those ideas with the spices and oils we saw yesterday. If we can find a small farm, we might be able to grow the plants needed and raise a few sheep to trade wool. Beyond that, I need to become a go-between and sell goods for the traders. That's the only way I can learn about the goods; how they are made and where they come from. We'll be merchants in no time."

"Slow down; you'll have me on one of those damn boats before I can blink. It makes me sick just thinking about it."

"It may not be so bad. I hear that there are short sea routes from Kent to France and East Angle to the Netherlands. From there, we would travel by land and see wonderful new places and find extraordinarily crafted goods to sell. Seafarers can then be paid to bring the items back to Britain whilst we take the land routes."

"How do you know all this?" I queried.

"Ah, some of it I have learned from listening to the traders, but a lot of things just seem to be in my mind. I have your master to thank for that. He may not have travelled out to sea, but he was a very learned man and must have acquired the knowledge over many years. Despite what I've been gifted, I still have a lot to learn about this world which seems to hold unlimited possibilities."

Chapter 12

When Audric set his mind to a particular plan, I never doubted that we would achieve his aims, and we made rapid progress in the next twelve months. Audric had saved coinage from our work on the northern abbeys, and this gave us a good start and some credibility with the locals.

Our first good fortune was to find a plot of land which had been farmed previously but had been in disuse for some time. The landowner was part of the noble classes, and he owned a large swathe of the countryside north of Lundenwic. Franco introduced us to the family, and they were pleased to get the land back in use.

We became tenant farmers, but the taxes would be waived for the next two years if we repaired or rebuilt the existing dwellings and reared a hundred sheep. We soon sorted out the dwellings with our skills and experience and probably had two of the best farm buildings in the region. Fifty young sheep were bought at a good price, and the rest would be achieved through breeding the following spring.

We both knew a good deal about farming, so we soon introduced pigs and geese and prepared the land for the seasons ahead. Winter was a challenge with cold, sharp frosts, and we had to buy in fodder for the animals and erect makeshift shelters to protect the livestock.

During the winter months, Audric discussed his progress with Baden, the landowner, and outlined our long-term plans to trade in goods other than just livestock. Baden had noted our building skills and asked if we could repair some of their more substantial stone buildings that dated back to Roman times and were now in poor condition. Baden was able to source old bits of stone from the partly dilapidated Londinium walls, and we soon raised a generous amount of coinage in carrying out the repairs.

Audric began to make a few purchases, mainly of silverware. He simply packed them up and hid the items in small crates buried in the ground. In return, Franco gave Audric lots of advice on where they were made and could be bought in the future, plus the sort of prices he might expect to pay.

By the following spring, we had settled in well; there were fewer cold mornings, and the lambing season was underway. By midsummer, we were shearing the sheep and bringing in the wool for sorting, though we could see already that our wool was of good quality. Each farmer baled his wool, and it was taken to a large timber shed run by merchants. Here the wool was checked and graded and then auctioned to the merchants by farmers experienced in the selling. As each lot was sold, the wool owner came forward to collect his coinage, though some wool passed through in exchange for pre-agreed goods held elsewhere. Our first dealings were in coinage, and we made a good return.

Twelve months on, we had more wealth, a secure home, a great deal more experience and many new friends. It was a different world from some of the hard times we had encountered on the road. We had a lot to be thankful for and held a small gathering on our farm to thank the locals for their support and friendship. We were praised for our enterprise and the progress in bringing the farm back to life. Discussions were now taking place to see what sort of partnership might be of benefit in future trading. Traders could tell that Audric had many new ideas that could help their trading, and he knew that they held the knowledge and skills to provide the goods. It became clear that some of the merchants were very wealthy and could finance large trading deals or new workshops. Audric locked all this information away in his mind for the future.

As the locals drifted away after enjoying our celebrations, I sat under a tree to gain shade from the sun.

"That was a great success," I shouted to Audric nearby. "Everyone seemed to enjoy the day. The merchant's wine probably helped the occasion and was better than we usually get to drink."

Audric agreed, "We've been lucky this last year, and it was good to celebrate in that way amongst our new friends."

"Remember a year ago we thought we were going into battle. It makes me cringe to think about it."

"Then you may not be happy at what I have to tell you."

"We're not leaving, are we?"

"No, at least I hope not."

"This sounds ominous."

"Well, I feel a little that way. I said I might have another premonition one day, and last night, it came in a dream. Wulfhere and his brother were on horseback leading a mighty army and seemed to be on a war footing. They camped near the old city walls of Londinium. I was hovering above and could see that Wulfhere was looking in distress. He looked at me intently, seemingly wondering where he had seen me before. He spoke the words, "Please help me." Wulfhere is going to cross our path again very soon, and we will not be able to avoid him. Whilst that doesn't mean we are in danger, he may wonder why we are here and not up north; and why I'm no longer a monk. To complicate matters, I sense that Wulfhere is destined to die within the year. That's a terrible thought to carry round in my head, even though he can be a man of violence."

"Can't we just disappear for a while when we see him arrive?"

"Sounds easy, but the premonition says we will meet, whether it is here or elsewhere. I can't change fate, and my dream didn't tell me what the outcome of our meeting will be - good or bad."

"He doesn't know that you were on a spying mission."

"Maybe, but he could work it out. His brother might remember seeing us inside the walls of Eoforwic even though we didn't confront him."

"Aye, I was down where they were tied up, checking they were being treated well. I never thought we might see them again."

"The Mercians control the kingdoms here, so he's likely to visit his realm from time to time to exert his power. Wulfhere will see this place as a potential source of wealth, or he may decide to use the land inside the Londinium walls to barrack his army and draw supplies from the local farms."

"So we sit and wait?"

"Well, carry on as normal, and I'll give the matter some thought."

"Just when I imagined life was all rosy."

"Keep smiling; we'll find a way around things."

"Or make a quick run for it after we've met Wulfhere again."

"Now, I'd never thought of that! Come on, let's tidy round."

Audric's news had spoilt what had been a wonderful day, but the food and drink helped me sleep well.

The next morning, I found Audric tending the garden where we were growing wildflowers, herbs and plants that we had lifted from the woods or grown from saplings provided by one of the traders.

"No more premonitions last night?" I asked.

"No, just a little unease at what is coming our way. I think it could be very soon."

"Are the plants growing well?"

"Not bad; they mature at different times. I'm checking what may be available as something tells me I might have a need for them, but let's wait and see. Your idea about running off might still be the best way out of trouble!"

"Then I'd better get a few things ready just in case."

I wandered off, leaving Audric to his thoughts as he rarely talked much when his mind was working on future plans.

We had a quiet few days and gradually put our worries to the back of our minds. I had prepared packs so we could ride off at speed and selected a route out through the nearby woods. Our hope was that we would come back later when the Mercians lost interest. Unexpectedly a rider came galloping in, and that set us on edge until we saw it was one of Baden's men.

He jumped from his horse and shouted enthusiastically, "Wulfhere is here at my Lords place. Apparently, his army is some distance away, camped up, but he has come in to see Baden. He seems unwell and resting up, but in some pain."

"How can we help?" queried Audric.

"Baden mentioned that he knew someone who occasionally treated a few of the locals down with illness using potions and gave them great relief."

"As you say, just a few, I'm no medicine man."

"The man looks very ill, and it might reflect badly on Baden if the king dies here."

Audric and I looked at each other, but I could see he had made up his mind. "We'll follow you back but give us time to collect a few things."

Audric explained that I didn't need to come along but asked if I could prepare a horse whilst he fetched his bag.

I prepared our horses and we followed Baden's man back to his master's hall.

As we approached, I could see about fifty of Wulfhere's men and the unmistakable figure of his brother, Æthelred. We were back in the lion's den, so I followed Audric's lead and rode in nonchalantly. Fortunately, we weren't recognised, and we were led to Baden's main dwelling and inside soon came across Wulfhere lying in bed. He looked up, and I sensed he recognised Audric but said nothing.

Audric took the initiative. "Where is your pain, Sire?"

The king rolled on his side with difficulty and put his hand on the right side of his stomach.

Audric put his hand over the same area, and Wulfhere flinched. "How long have you had these lumps?"

"Several months, but I have coped with the pain until a few weeks ago."

"Have you coughed up any blood?" continued Audric.

"A little to begin with, but more of late."

"Can you eat and drink?"

"Eating has become more difficult, but I'm always thirsty now."

"Can I speak to you alone, Sire?"

Wulfhere thought for a moment, then waved for those standing around to leave them alone. I joined the exodus.

Outside there was a lot of whispering until a while later, Audric emerged. He walked past the small gathering, out of the dwelling and went straight over to Æthelred. He took him aside and talked at length before passing over a small bag and then gave Wulfhere's brother a friendly hug.

Audric returned to our steads. We rode off in silence until a short while later, Audric said, "Wulfhere is dying and may only have a few weeks to live. He recognised me as the young monk but seemed content to trust me and believe in me as a man of God. I have provided enough medicine to relieve the pain in the coming weeks and suggested he stay with Baden. Your master passed on sufficient experience for me to understand the king has several growths that will eat him up from the inside. On this occasion, there will be no miracle cure, and I cannot help further. Wulfhere has accepted his fate and already guessed he was dying. We will only attend him again if he calls for us. AEthelred will take his place as king."

"You have great compassion; perhaps you should become a monk."

"Life's not that easy as I'm not sure I believe in God. There should be compassion inside us all, but it doesn't mean we have to put aside our own ambitions and desires. There is much to be excited about in the real world for the moment. Maybe God will come to me later."

"Perhaps God bought you back to Wulfhere's side in his time of need."

"You are too wise for me today, Tork."

"Then let me lead on, and we can drink that bottle of wine I hid away the other day."

"You get wiser by the day, and there should be no need to ride away from trouble. We may even have friends in both camps now."

What had seemed about to bring our lives tumbling down had been turned on its head.

Chapter 13

W e returned to the farm where there was still plenty to do, and finished the day with a generous amount of wine left over from the earlier celebrations with friends.

A few days passed, and normality, returned leaving us happy and content again until two riders appeared at a gallop, and we recognised AEthelred and one of his guards. He dismounted and took Audric aside. They spoke for a short while before AEthelred shook Audric's hand and left as quickly as he had arrived.

I wandered over to Audric's side, "So what did he have to say?"

"Wulfhere has passed away. AEthelred says there will be three days of mourning, and then AEthelred becomes King. He offered thanks for helping his brother die in peace without too much pain. The brothers spoke of their past together and how AEthelred might reign in the future. I had wondered why the army had come to Lundenwic, and my fears have been confirmed. The Mercians plan to take control of Kent to extend their kingdom even further."

"How much land does any man need?" I replied.

"I told AEthelred to look around and see how prosperity had followed peace in the area and asked why disturb things, but he is determined on his power grab."

"I imagine he and his brother were shaken by their defeat in Northumbria, and this is a chance to show they're still a force to be reckoned with."

"It may go further than taking Kent. The new king reminded me that the vow of peace with Northumbria will no longer apply now his brother is dead. I think it rankles with him that their defeat was due to his capture."

"The Northumbrians will soon know of Wulfhere's death and will be more prepared than ever. Next time Aldren and Oldred will be able to call on the Northumbria King for more support."

Audric was saddened. "There is nothing I can do this time. We just need to get on with our lives here and hope not to get involved."

Four days later, we were tending the livestock when AEthelred led his army through Lundenwic.

"God help the people of Rochester and Canterbury," I thought. I watched the procession, but Audric barely turned his head. He appeared calm and unconcerned, but I was sure he was overcome with anger after our efforts in Eoforwic to maintain peace.

The months passed through to winter again, and I reflected on the progress made on the farm.

"We have six score sheep now," I said to Audric during our walk around the farm past the new buildings erected to house livestock in the extreme cold weather. "That should double our wool sales next year."

"The wool's fetching good prices," replied Audric, "especially from the overseas merchants. They like the quality."

All this was increasing our wealth rapidly, but I could see Audric's long term vision was to become a merchant and maybe see the world.

"I still dread the idea of going to sea after hearing stories of boats wrecked offshore or leaving the port and never being seen again."

"Most boats return to port time and again, and the merchants persist with their efforts to trade widely because there is great wealth to be made. They surround themselves with experienced men, those that understand the risks and can look after themselves when needed."

We were not ready to trade goods yet, though Audric had acquired many valuable items which we had buried, mainly at night and used our ingenuity to disguise the places. Other treasures were wrapped in straw and laid up in our dwellings. He would come back after market days and show me the wonderful pieces he had bought and talk enthusiastically about them. I would show great interest and could see why Audric appreciated them.

"How do you know you'll make coinage on the items purchased?" I asked Audric one evening.

"There's no guarantee, but I'm beginning to recognise quality workmanship, and Franco feels I've paid fair prices that should show good returns."

Despite his ambitions, Audric stuck to our routines and worked hard on the farm, as well as learning new trading skills. It was as if he had to experience all walks of life before chasing his ambitions, and so he was in no great hurry to pursue his adventurous spirit.

With snow on the ground, there was little to be done as another harsh winter took a grip and traders were rarely seen. Feeding the livestock and keeping them safe was our lot in these conditions, and there was little excitement until one day when worn out and badly injured warriors started to pass through Lundenwic.

We soon learnt that the Mercians had successfully taken Kent but not without many being killed or maimed. Most of the army were staying in Kent until the opposing kings reached an agreement on control of the kingdom, which usually meant taking over swathes of land and prime properties. Sometimes young, single men from the defeated army were made to vow allegiance to the conquering king and join his army.

Those passing through were returning home to their families where they would be better cared for, but I sensed some would not survive the journey. Those who did get home might wonder if the battle was worth the losses and injuries suffered.

This time Audric did watch them pass by and looked on with sadness and sympathy.

I looked to console him, "Thank goodness we avoided this in Eoforwic."

"It's tragic, Tork. Look at the injured men. The carnage on the battlefield must have been horrific."

"Aye, and you think they may head for Northumbria next?"

"If the losses are as they seem, then it could be some time before they risk going north again."

"Just a matter of time then?"

"I fear so. Let's see if we can help any of the injured."

We walked amongst the wounded, and most had their injuries well bound. Here and there, a few were in great pain, so Audric gave them the same pain relief given to Wulfhere. Also, some appeared dehydrated, and we fetched water. Others required fresh dressings, so we found clean linen, and Audric added some powder which he said would reduce the risk of infection. The Mercians barely stopped for their help, but we threw in bits of food where it seemed most in need and watched them disappear into the distance. It took a while before we could turn our attention back to the farm, and by then, the snow was wiping out any sign that the injured men had passed through.

Strangely it made me think about the battlefields I had seen in years gone by. Nothing could obliterate those from my memory.

Audric broke my thoughts, "Back to the sheep. They may need extra feed if the snow continues to fall. You do that, and I'll check the horses are secure and fed. Then I need a drink to lift my mood."

The snow fell all night but had stopped by morning. The sky was a brilliant blue, and the surroundings a complete whiteout, with just a couple of small trails where wild animals must have strayed looking for food. The snow was knee-deep as we cleared an area around the dwellings and shelters where the lambs were huddled with a haze forming as warm air came off their bodies and cooled above them. The scene of beauty did not hide the harshness that the winter was bringing to us for the second year in a row. Hard frosts would follow, and we'd need to endure long cold days. We were well prepared, but the days seemed long with plenty of time to think. After recent events, that was not what we really needed, so I began to relate my early recollections of my master.

"I was a young man when I first met him," I began, "but unlike you, I have no memory of my childhood and Master insisted he was not my father. He had found me unconscious or asleep one day, and whilst he could tell I was not dead, it was a few days before I came round. I knew nothing of my past or how I had got to the woods where you first saw our home. As I've mentioned on our journey, I've never met any dwarfs like myself, so I naturally stayed with Morgan and started to call him Master because he taught me so much and cared for me.

"When I was about your present age, he told me I could leave home to make my own way in life and do what suited me best, but I decided to stay. I continued to call him Master out of habit, though he said I could call him Morgan if I wished. We lived in the same home all his life and travelled to many places, but never overseas. The first sign of his special ways arose when one day, we were cornered by a group of people who were curious about my size. Whilst it was playful, to begin with, things started to get nasty with taunting and attempts to steal Master's bags which contained many of his potions. Suddenly Master swivelled around, and before anyone could move, he was behind the rogues. They were wondering where he was whilst I could see him standing behind them.

"At first, I thought he had moved faster than the eye could follow, but as remarkable as that would be, Master later explained that he had the power to momentarily freeze time for those around him whilst he continued to move. He also pointed out that these instances only occurred instinctively when danger arose, and he could not repeat them like magic tricks.

"Anyway, before they guessed what had happened, one was on the floor with Master's foot on the man's chest. Another threw a blow with a heavy baton but inexplicably missed Master by a long way and ended up on the ground in mud that I don't remember being there in the first place. The third man looked threatening, but Master stared back, and the man turned and ran off. I sat on the man in the mud, and Master asked them if they wanted to continue. They soon ran off, and we looked at each other and laughed. Other far more serious incidents occurred, including getting caught up in battlefields, but more of that another time."

"I remember my parents well," Audric responded. "They had a difficult life, working the land and moving from one settlement to another. My father was a strong man, and he would often lift me above his head in a playful manner and say, 'Who's the chief around here?' He made me laugh a lot and taught me to ride and hunt wild animals. I also helped on the farm, and as I turned ten years old, I could manage most jobs as well as a man.

"What about your mother?" I asked, not having had a mother who cared for me.

"My mother was kind and looked after us all, making clothes, cooking and keeping the home warm. There was none of the wealth we are starting to see, and working the land was our life. Travelling from one settlement to another seemed to be in the blood, and maybe that is still part of my desire for adventure nowadays."

"How did you get separated from your parents?"

"One day, there was shouting and screaming, and it was soon clear that the settlement was under attack. I was away from our dwelling, working and playing with a friend. His parents grabbed us by our arms and shouted to run for the woods. We were lucky to reach the woods and hid in the undergrowth. Screaming continued in the distance before finally subsiding. We moved further into the woods and well away from the settlement."

"You must have felt desperate at that point."

"I wanted to run back, but I was restrained. The following morning, we moved slowly back to the edge of the wood and watched for some time until we were sure the attackers had gone. We walked towards some of the dwellings, passing several dead bodies on the way and could see others in the distance. Tears welled up in our eyes as we recognised some of the bodies, and I fully expected to find my father and mother amongst the dead."

"What happened to them?"

"Another couple of the settlers we knew also came out of the woods and joined us. Our search of the settlement revealed twenty dead bodies and several still alive with serious injuries. The attackers had ransacked the buildings and taken all the livestock, produce and anything else they thought useful. Some of the survivors said others had fled, but many had been taken and bound by rope and led away. They were too shocked and distressed to know who was taken or who might have escaped. From that day, I never stopped looking for my parents as there seemed to be a reasonable chance they might be alive, but as time went on, I gave up hope."

"That must have been terrible for an eleven-year-old boy. How did you cope?"

"I was well cared for by the travellers who rescued me, but I had nightmares for months after. Gradually I settled back into the routine of the farm and stayed with them until I felt the urge to travel and seek some kind of adventure. I think I was looking for my parents again, but it wasn't long before I came across your home in the woods. Your master seemed to suggest my arrival was preordained and based on what has happened since I think there is truth in his words."

I let his words settle and then said, "I'm pleased that we have got to know each other so well, but your story is very sad. I hope that one day you find your parents again."

"I haven't given up hope, but it does seem unlikely after all this time."

As it turned out, it was the last snow of that winter, but the frosts were hard. Large parts of the River Thames froze over, leaving areas where people felt it safe to entertain themselves by sliding and walking on the ice. However, it seemed precarious in parts where the ice looked thin and was cracking as water passed beneath. Collecting water was no easy matter - we either had to melt the snow or break through the ice-covered wells and ponds. Our wool-lined leather jackets and new boots were a godsend, but we walked around smelling of smoke from our fires which we kept alight most of the time. Washing ourselves was a rare treat in winter, often with a warm damp cloth and sometimes using the snow if we had been working hard collecting more firewood.

The first signs of spring around the corner saw ice melting and dripping off the branches and the last patches of snow disappearing into the ground. Most of the sheep had survived the winter and they would be released onto the fields soon. Barely had our minds turned towards the lambing season when a small group of riders came into view and looked familiar. Their robes soon became clear, and the monks rode towards us with Abbot Wilfrid bringing up the rear.

Audric walked over and helped the abbot down from his horse. He seemed worn out and stiff from time in the saddle.

"Thank you," said Abbot Wilfrid. "It's good to see you both again, especially after our long journey."

"We never imagined we'd see you down this way; what brings you to Lundenwic?" asked Audric.

"There is a story to tell, but first, could we seek shelter here and a little food and drink? My assistants can erect a tent for their use, but I would welcome a bunk for the night. I am getting too old for these hard grounds, especially during the recent winter months."

"Tork will help the monks set up over by our dwelling, and I will get you settled inside. If you need some sleep, we will give you some food then leave you to rest."

"Thank you," said the abbot. "That will be very welcome."

We left them to rest and pondered how they had found us and why they were here.

Abbot Wilfrid slept from evening till dawn the next day, clearly washed out from his recent travels, but was up early, and we all sat down to eat.

"That was some sleep," said the abbot, "and I must thank you again. You deserve an explanation for our falling on your dwelling without warning. It has been a difficult time for me and the other monks who support my religious aims."

"Take your time, Abbot; there is no rush, but who told you we were in Lundenwic?"

"Æthelred says he met you here when his brother died, and then he appears to have taken Kent by storm. He is back in Trent, and I called in there to get his support. The king was unable to visit you on his return but sends his best wishes and hopes you can provide me with a little help on my way to Canterbury."

"If we are able," replied Audric, "but why do you need Æthelred's support?"

"Ecgfrith, the Northumbrian king, has come out in favour of Theodore, the Archbishop of Canterbury, who wishes to move away from many of the ways that guide the Church of Rome. Theodore also wants to create more dioceses by splitting up the existing diocese. That way, he can appoint further bishops and gain their favour. I have argued with Ecgfrith, but he is adamant, and he has expelled me even though he has no such authority. That authority lies with the pope or members of a council he can convene from senior churchmen in Britain. I lose control of Hexham and Ripon and seem unlikely to regain my appointment as Bishop of Eoforwic."

"The nobility appears to be meddling with church affairs," suggested Audric.

"I'm afraid so, and that is why I turned to Æthelred. I am not looking to regain my position by force, but I hoped he could influence the church in the southern kingdoms to maintain the ways of the Church of Rome. He has helped by appointing me Bishop of Middle Angles, but for the unity of the Church, I need to persuade Theodore to recant his ideas. He is currently residing in Canterbury, so I will travel down to see him."

"How can we help you?"

"You have already helped, and I have learnt over time of your good counsel. I wondered if you would escort me to Canterbury and support my case. I don't want to create the wrong impression and ride in with Æthelred's warriors, and you have more subtle ways to deal with difficult situations."

"We would be happy to escort you through Kent, but I will have to think more about the help you seek to change church matters. I think the best I might offer would be to ensure you receive a fair hearing."

"You are already showing good counsel in reminding me of my duty to the Church and not just my ego, so I look forward to our journey to Canterbury.

Abbot Wilfrid took an extra day's rest whilst we organised for the neighbouring farm to watch over our livestock until we returned, hopefully within seven to ten days. Abbot Wilfrid carried the king's seal so, should we come across the remains of the Mercian army, we would be safe enough. The aim was to pass through Rochester and stay there the night. The abbot hoped we would be well received by the church there, but the town was apparently ravaged by the Mercian army, and it was difficult to know what to expect.

Our journey to Rochester was easy enough, and we passed remnants of the Mercian army making their way home as well as what appeared to be some dispossessed families seeking a new life elsewhere. We made our destination by early evening after a hard ride and little rest. There was still evidence of the battle that had taken place: some buildings partially destroyed and newly dug graves, but this was nothing compared to the carnage that must have taken place on the first day of attack. There was still fear in the faces of the people in the streets, and they stayed well clear of us, despite the monks' appearance.

We passed by the old Roman walls, and the church came in view. However, instead of a picture of tranquillity, the church was partially in ruin. Sections of the walls lay demolished, and it had clearly been attacked, probably because some of the defeated army had sought refuge in the buildings. As we got closer, it was evident the church had been ransacked with debris scattered around the grounds. There had been little respect for the church on this occasion. Abbot Wilfrid continued around the grounds until we came to a few dwellings away from the church and a monk came out to greet us. We dismounted and the abbot spoke at length to the monk before coming over to speak to us.

"The Mercians showed no mercy when the people of Rochester retreated to the church, and even unarmed men were slain. It would seem that the Mercian army simply went on a rampage, and their leaders had little control of their men at the height of the battle. Fortunately, when King AEthelred entered the town, a degree of order was restored, and he put protection in place around the church grounds. The church school and the monks' dwellings have remained untouched, and we can rest there until we are ready to move on."

"Is there anything we can do to help the people?" asked Audric.

"The people are grieving their lost ones and are in fear that the Mercians will attack again. It will take a long time to return to normal life here. It would seem that Canterbury escaped the same degree of carnage by surrendering early and conceding to the demands of King AEthelred. He has left overlords and their men to ensure the Kent kingdom remains submissive and carries out his orders."

"It's a great pity that Wulfhere died," I suggested. "His brother has a far more ruthless streak."

Audric retorted, "I'm not sure there is much to choose between them. The battle for supremacy throughout the kingdoms is their way of life; why else do they carry out these raids? They have no respect for life and the real joys it can bring."

That comment brought silence, and we just drifted off to fasten up our horses nearby. A monk led the way into the school building and then on the corridor to three small bunk rooms for the abbot, Audric and me. Abbot Wilfrid's other monks were taken elsewhere, and we congregated later in a dining hall with about twenty other monks for a simple meal. The conversation was subdued, and it was difficult to talk about anything else other than the way Rochester had been ravaged.

I broke the silence, "Two hundred local men have been buried and many injured, according to a monk I spoke with earlier. Some people have scattered to the countryside and they may be afraid to return."

"It breaks my heart to hear those words," replied Audric.

"Some families have since left Rochester in the hope of finding peace elsewhere or reuniting with families in other parts," announced the abbot.

With a degree of despair, Audric excused us from the table, and we wandered out into the streets.

Audric wanted to see the port side and the location of the trader's market, but we doubted the sites would show much activity after the current turmoil. That proved to be the case with the market completely bare and the port largely devoid of larger boats that probably took to sea at the first signs of trouble. It might be some time before confidence would be restored and the traders returned. We had heard that the movement of boats from these docks was one of the best places to work from, but it wouldn't be possible to make serious enquiries at the moment. At least we had seen the position for ourselves and would need to bide our time.

We assumed there would be little to keep the abbot in Rochester and that we'd be on the road to Canterbury tomorrow. Back at the bunk rooms, Abbot Wilfrid confirmed he would like to set off in the morning and aim to get to Canterbury before dark.

Our journey the next day was uneventful, though we were stopped by Mercian army men once but soon allowed on our way after cursory checks. As we neared Canterbury, there were more warriors watching the road, but we passed unhindered, and on entering the town, we saw less of the devastation seen in Rochester. There were still worried faces and not many people on the streets.

The church was slightly bigger than Rochester and appeared older but not as grand as that being built in Ripon. The grounds had a few other buildings, and the surrounding area was densely packed with mainly timber dwellings but also stone buildings, possibly constructed in Roman times.

We rode over to one of the larger stone buildings with a small courtyard which soon revealed itself as a place of importance. Monks were moving around purposefully, and two came to welcome us, seeming to recognise Abbot Wilfrid as they held his horse whilst he dismounted.

"Wait here whilst I explain our presence," requested Abbot Wilfrid.

He returned shortly. "The archbishop will see us tomorrow. In the meantime, we have been given a bunkhouse big enough for all of us, and dinner will be served when the bell rings."

The room had four single bunks, a table and two benches and a chest of drawers topped with a couple of basins of water. You couldn't say the monks were ever spoilt and what we had noticed was there rarely seemed to be a fire, or even a hearth, in the bunkrooms. On the farm, we kept the fire on the go all day during colder spells. Would we get a warm welcome tomorrow? The progress of Audric and I had been closely related to that of Abbot Wilfrid, and we had grown fond of him, but his position seemed very similar to the power games between the warring kingdoms. In some ways, it gave the kings further reasons to go to war to secure land and status. I wondered which way Audric would lean this time.

Chapter 14

The following morning, we made our way to the archbishop's residence, a short distance from the church. The rooms we passed showed signs of comfort and wealth but were not overly ostentatious. Abbot Wilfrid had asked that Audric and I both attend along with his own assistant, and clearly, there was to be a degree of formality involved.

Archbishop Theodore was an elderly man and looked impressive in his religious robes. We sat around a large circular table when the archbishop greeted us.

"Welcome, Abbot Wilfrid. It's some time since we last met and several years on from when I first appointed you Bishop of Eoforwic. I'm sorry that we meet in such difficult circumstances, but it is important that the Church in England moves on as it grows. I did not wish to remove you from your position, but I feel reforms are necessary. King Ecgfrith also intervened, and you seem to have lost his support, making matters more difficult for the Church."

The archbishop paused, and Abbot Wilfrid took up his defence.

"Your support in recent years has been unwavering, and in return, I have discharged my episcopal duties with great diligence. Monasteries have been founded, churches built, and the Christian faith has grown rapidly, both amongst the common people and the nobility. To lose all that seems a harsh reward for my services."

Archbishop Theodore looked on sympathetically and replied, "This has not come about in one fell swoop, and the changes sought have been explained over recent years. Part of this is due to your own success. Your diocese is very large now, and throughout England, there is a need to create more dioceses and give other ordained men, who have been well-schooled, the opportunity to be bishops. It is also the size of your diocese that seems to concern the king and what he sees as the power you may hold."

Looking slightly aggrieved, Abbot Wilfrid answered, "Surely my experience and hard work deserve a diocese of some size, and there is a lot I can still do to grow Christianity throughout Northumbria and England."

"There are other issues as well, Wilfrid. Your rigorous allegiance to the Church of Rome is to be commended, but not all customs are welcome or supported within the Church here. There is a need to accept customs that best suit Christianity in England. The rule of the pope isn't so easily accepted here without query."

"Surely," expressed Abbot Wilfrid, "the unity and lead provided by Rome are important to lay the foundations for Christianity as it grows in England. The customs are the basis of Christ's teachings."

Archbishop Theodore looked slightly irritated at these words. "Not everyone agrees with your views, and unity can only be achieved when consensus is reached. In my position as leader of the Church of England, it is my duty to gain all-round support if we want Christianity to succeed here. The lead given by Rome is important, but it must acknowledge local circumstances; otherwise, the people will eventually return to paganism."

Audric had listened carefully and seemed unready to intervene until Abbot Wilfrid turned his way.

"Archbishop Theodore knows how I have grown to respect your judgement. Do you have any words that may help?"

"I rely on my vivid imagination and rational thought when I seek solutions to problems confronted. When I visualise the future, I can only see King Ecgfrith reinforcing his position of power and seeking to reduce that of the Church. He sees you, Abbot, as a powerful man with control over large areas of land and its people through the Christian faith. Success in your work only makes the king more suspicious. I have imagined Northumbria in a years' time and don't foresee your presence. I can sense that the archbishop will have achieved consensus by dividing your See amongst several clergymen, which the king will feel is less of a risk. Whilst that may seem unfair, I do visualise your time in Rome being a challenge that reinforces your faith and will allow you to be reinstated on your return."

Abbot Wilfrid looked unsettled, but from his silence, I sensed the end had come for now.

Theodore pondered how to bring matters to a close and began slowly. "Dear Wilfrid, I have great respect for you and didn't remove you from your position lightly. I think you were right to say your friend gives good counsel, as my thoughts were that we would not be able to reconcile our differences. If you choose to go to Rome and seek papal guidance, it may be that time will prove useful in our dealings with Ecgfrith. In addition, if the pope supports your cause, then that could lead to your reinstatement. Otherwise, I'm aware you have been appointed Bishop to Middle Angles by AEthelred, and I will not challenge that, even though it isn't within his right to make that appointment. I am sure we can work together in common purpose for the good of the Church."

Abbot Wilfrid still looked aggrieved. "I know I should be humble and seek the common good, but the loss of all I have created hurts, and I feel the work in Northumbria is unfinished. I'm minded to go to Rome and hope one day my position as Bishop of Eoforwic can be restored. I can see that Ecgfrith's intervention has made my position impossible at the moment."

The archbishop looked relieved and seemed to have genuine feelings for Abbot Wilfrid. "Then I support your journey to Rome and will provide you with an entourage commensurate with that of a bishop. Might I ask Audric a question?"

The abbot nodded.

"What are your plans for the future? The Church could do with young blood and a mind like your own. You do not need to be religious, just compassionate and a man of reason."

"Thank you for your interest, but I don't wish to be bound by the nobility or the Church. Although, I am happy to work alongside both for the good of the nation and its people. I hope, in time, you are able to use Abbot Wilfrid to good cause and meet his ambitions."

Archbishop Theodore looked to draw matters to a close. "You seem to have turned Abbot Wilfrid and me full circle with good intent. May you enjoy your journey in life."

I reflected that Audric might have been imbued with my former masters' experiences, but he had his own very remarkable way with people.

We retreated to our bunkhouse, and little was said on the walk back. Abbot Wilfrid was pensive and Audric, and I strolled on slightly behind to allow him time for his thoughts.

Once settled, Abbot Wilfrid looked at Audric and said, "I can't deny I was surprised not to receive your full support, but I can see that the end result would probably have been no different. A journey to Rome will be physically demanding at my age but should rejuvenate my mind. Maybe I have become complacent and lost sight of the needs of the Church."

Audric sought to console him. "We all need to step back occasionally and look at ourselves. You have had a remarkable life so far, and can be very proud of your work. The future may be different to what you expected, but it can be both challenging and exciting."

"I wish I had your youthful enthusiasm, though as I think about it, I am excited by the prospect of returning to Rome. When I returned to England after my last journey to Rome, there was much to be done. I was full of ideas, and many have come to fruition. You're right; I need to refresh my mind and seek new ways."

"Tork and I will make ready to return to Lundenwic and leave shortly. I hope we will meet again in slightly better circumstances."

"God bless you both."

We were ready to go back to our home in Lundenwic, having missed the routine of looking after the farm and talking with the friends we had made there. The strain of passing through war-torn Rochester made it seem like more than the three days we had been away. We didn't look forward to seeing the sorry sights in the town again, but we felt it was important we didn't turn our backs on what had happened there.

We decided to camp outside Rochester rather than stay with the monks there, and then we rode in by early evening to look again at the devastation caused. We spoke with a few families who had returned to their homes, and though they were a little suspicious of our visit, they thanked us for our concern. Some had lost their menfolk and seemed at a loss as to what to do next: whether to stay or move on. Audric decided we should remain for a while and provide help where we could.

During the following week, we organised the farms into groups, ensuring there was sufficient physical support for each farm. Simple repairs were carried out, and what livestock hadn't been taken by the Mercians was secured and shared out to ensure food and milk all-around. We helped set in place the work needed to complete some of the more major repairs. Gradually the town folk took control as the shock of the battle receded, and they saw purpose in their lives again, grieving together whilst they restored their homes. Audric identified a few of the men he could trust and left them with sufficient coinage to overcome any hardship the people of the town might suffer during the next few days.

We left when there seemed little more we could do in the short term. We promised to visit again in the coming months and offered them shelter if they came to Lundenwic. There were still Mercian warriors in and passing through Rochester, but they seemed to keep to themselves and didn't hinder the townsfolk as they tried to rebuild their lives. Returning to the relative serenity of Lundenwic and seeing our farm settlement was a real joy, though nothing had changed. Our neighbours were pleased to see us, and they had tended to the farm well in our absence.

Audric looked happy to be back. "How are you feeling after that journey, Tork? It's not the sort of adventure I've been seeking, but I've learnt a lot from the experience."

"Aye," I said, "it's a relief to be home again, and it looks like lambing is underway, so we'll be busy in the coming weeks."

"Let's give the horses some feed and water; then we'll wander around the farm.

"It's difficult not to think of the poor folk in Rochester. In some ways, we are lucky that the Mercians already control this kingdom; otherwise, we might have suffered the same carnage as Kent."

"War is a part of our age, and there is little we can do about it. As you say, it is a matter of good fortune to avoid being involved. If the stories we hear from the merchants are to be believed, then it is no better elsewhere."

"How do we rid ourselves of these depressing thoughts?"

"Try to embrace life where we can, and look to stay one step ahead of the warmongers. Sometimes there is no choice other than to stand and fight, but a wise man will choose the time and place."

"And where is our place at the moment?"

"You ask difficult questions, Tork. Will the southern kingdoms rise against the Mercians and drive them out? I would guess that we are safe for a year or so, but invaders from overseas could attack at any time. There seem to be more and more boats reaching our shores, and they could bring warriors in increasing numbers."

"We could end up running from one place to another to avoid trouble."

"Eventually, we have to resist, but there is no point in taking on a lost cause; better to live and fight another day. There is no single answer to your question - we need to keep our wits about us. The kingdoms may need to unite to defeat a serious invasion from overseas."

After those sad reflections, we returned to our work on the farm, and Audric continued to collect new items from the traders and merchants. We heard news from travellers that the people of Rochester were settling back to normal life, and trading was picking up with more and more boats coming into port. The markets were busy, and former settlers had returned to their farms when the risks seemed safe again. Lundenwic was also becoming very busy: the number of workshops was increasing and the range of goods on the markets widening. Audric had purchased several beautiful glass containers brought in from Italy. With summer around the corner, Audric was talking of commencing trading from Lundenwic and Rochester, plus visiting certain of the nobility homes.

I liked to wander around the markets on my own whilst Audric considered his purchases, sometimes imagining I was buying goods for our collection. I also watched the people to see what sort could afford to buy such goods; very few came from the farm settlements.

Then one day, I saw the unmistakable figures of Canu and his father, Elred.

I instinctively shouted out, "Canu!" momentarily forgetting that Canu was deaf.

Elred looked my way then smiled before turning Canu to face me. An enormous smile passed over Canu's face, and then he ran over to hug me.

I made a few signs that we had improvised in our time in Hexham, and then I turned to Elred. "It's wonderful to see you both. What are you doing here?"

Elred's face saddened a little. "My wife died a few months ago, and then my son Gavin left to join with the Northumbrian forces, deciding against farming for a living. It wasn't easy then to work the farm, so we thought to try our luck elsewhere. We had heard of Lundenwic and its thriving activities and have slowly made our way down, working here and there to gain food and shelter. We have a horse and cart and have pulled up a short distance away until we find a place to stay. How is Audric?"

"He's fine. You must come and stay with us until you are sorted. Audric is around the market somewhere. He has a liking for some of the exotic goods you see on some of the stalls."

"Then he must be doing better than when I first saw you?"

"A lot has happened since then, and Audric has shown himself to be very resourceful. He will be delighted to see you both. Come, show me where your cart is, and I'll take you to our farm."

Canu still had a big grin on his face, and we set off to get the horse and cart. Then we rode back to the farm and soon caught sight of Audric carrying a small bag of goods. He turned on hearing the cart and, on seeing us, gave out a playful shout. We ate and drank to celebrate our reunion and told Elred they should stay as long as they wished. There was work to do on the farm, and Audric briefly explained that he and I might want to spend time away.

We found out that Elred's wife died of a fever which the rest of the family were lucky not to catch. Gavin was affected by the loss of his mother, and that's what seemed to drive him away to seek something new. He had grown into a strapping young man, so the nobles were glad to take him within their ranks, and he had not been seen since. They had no real thoughts as to what they would do but would welcome work on the farm.

Audric spent more and more time away from the farm. He was mostly engaged in long conversations with various traders and merchants, not just learning how things worked but also suggesting new ideas. His main suggestion was the establishment of a consortium of traders and, in the long term, the building of an indoor forum hall where goods could be auctioned to the highest bidder. Prior to the auction, goods would be displayed in cabinets or on shelves. Security of the building would be achieved using guards paid for by the consortium.

Not everyone was taken with the ideas, but several were very keen, seeing it as a way of enhancing trade by drawing the nobility and wealthy merchants from further afield. Lundenwic would become the prime place to visit for this type of trading, and it would work well with the port, which was becoming increasingly important. The number of people living in the area seemed to have doubled since our arrival, and plots of land were being made available by the landowners for many uses, not just farming. Audric was convinced that Lundenwic, and possibly the unoccupied land inside the Roman walls, would soon become one of the most important places in Britain for trading, including the movement of goods in and out of the country.

Chapter 15

As we moved into late summer, Audric's suggestions were being wholeheartedly supported, and many of the traders and merchants had banded together to form a consortium. The building would be constructed from a combination of spare stone from the Londinium walls and oak from the nearby woods. Adjoining the building, there was to be a large storage shed where pens could hold the sheep for sale or trade. The road down to the docks was to be improved to ensure smooth movement of the haulage. The aim was to complete the building work before winter and be ready the following spring to begin trading.

A selected group of traders were chosen to decide the priority of goods to go on display, but all traders would get a fair share of space and time to show their wares. Coinage was becoming increasingly available, with silver-based coins being struck in newly founded mints in Londinium and Rochester. This was making it easier for merchants and traders to buy or sell goods. The nobility and wealthy landowners could see the progress should increase their wealth and gave their support to the plans. All in all, the plans were ambitious and would create enormous change, even for the peasants who could see the demand for their wool increasing and prices rising.

Audric and I spent less time on the farm, leaving Elred and Canu to run things whilst we used our building experience to get the Forum underway. The building progressed at a great pace as many temporary workers joined the work.

By late autumn, the exterior was completed and the building weatherproof. We celebrated by having a grand fete with food and drink. Several market stalls sold donated goods to raise coinage towards fitting out the interior. The Forum was now the centrepiece for Lundenwic and would attract people from far and wide.

Audric and I looked on with pride at the building, having put an enormous effort into its construction. This prompted me to ask, "What are we to do with our time now? The farm's in good hands and the building's completed."

"We deserve a rest and to let our limbs recover. Let's walk down to the port. I'd like to see the type of boats that are coming and going at the moment."

"Oh aye, that rest wouldn't involve a trip out to sea, I hope!"

"Not yet, we have a lot to do to make sure the Forum is a success before thinking about travelling overseas, but we need to understand what's coming into port. New boats and people seem to come in all the time, and a few stay to ply their trade here. We can both help and learn from these foreigners."

"It's hard to believe the amount of change since we arrived. It's like a different world."

"I sometimes dream of that different world. The places I see are often very exotic - unlike anything I have ever seen in my lifetime. One such vision was filled with people in long white robes and matching headdresses that protect them from the intense heat that their country seems to experience - far more intense than we suffer, even in our hottest summers. They wear precious jewellery, and many of the women are clothed in beautiful silk garments. Despite the heat, the surrounding land has plenty of greenery and unusual trees. The market stalls display exotic fruits as well as goods suggesting high levels of sophistication and prosperity."

"You paint a wonderful picture, but are these places real?"

"They certainly seem real, and we occasionally hear stories from the foreign merchants that add credence to what I have visualised. When we have the wealth and experience, then I hope we can explore such places and find out for ourselves."

We reached the riverside, which seemed busier than ever and strolled from boat to boat. Audric occasionally asked the sailors what goods they carried and where they were from. He was interested in how long their journeys took and if boats could be hired with their crew.

Suddenly there was a high-pitched scream, and we turned in the direction of the voice. We couldn't immediately see anything, so we dashed down to the water's edge. In the river, a short distance out, a small child was splashing about and moving slowly along with the flow of the water. I was about to dive into the water, but Audric held me back. He ran a short distance downriver and knelt down. Time seemed to stand still, and the water became calm and ceased to flow. Then Audric grabbed a wooden crate, jumped into the river and swam towards the child, who now appeared in less distress. The moment seemed to have passed, and the river was in flow again, but Audric and the child were closing in on the riverside. They reached a timber post and held tight. I was then able to reach down from a ladder and lift the child out. Audric somehow scrambled out unnoticed as I attended to the child, who was a young boy, maybe ten years old.

"How's the boy?" asked Audric.

"He's just coughed up some water, but he looks like he'll survive. How are you? Was it my imagination, or did something special happen there?"

"There was a moment, maybe; I don't really remember. You can tell me later when the boy is safe."

The boy opened his eyes and spluttered again, looking fearful of my presence, as if I had been responsible for his fall into the river.

To reassure the boy, I said, "You're safe now. How are you feeling? Can you sit up?"

I lifted him up slightly, and he seemed to settle as he looked around.

Audric stood by and smiled. "Do you belong to a boat, or did you fall off the decking?"

The boy replied in words we didn't understand and shrugged his shoulders. As with Canu, I used some improvised signs. I pointed at Audric and did some exaggerated swimming strokes. Then I pointed at him and after at the boats near where he must have fallen in. He nodded his head and began to stand up, then pointed his arm at a large boat a little way back upriver. The boy was smart; he quickly took us both by the hand and pulled us towards the boat.

As we neared the side of the vessel, a man came on the deck of the boat and was taken aback to see us all. He shouted at the boy, who replied with equal vigour whilst pointing at us both. Relief crossed the man's face, and he scrambled off the boat and ran to pick up the boy.

Audric spoke a few words I didn't understand, then added, "The boy seems well now."

The man responded, "I can speak in your native language. I've travelled here many times and worked on farms hereabouts. Thank you for rescuing my son. When they get to his age, you think they can start to look after themselves. I'll need to take more care and hope he has learnt not to take too many risks. My name is Perron and the boy, Gabriel. Our homeland is France, but we have spent time in Brittany, where many Britons have sought refuge over the years."

Audric explained who we were and how we lived locally.

That prompted Perron, "Are you involved with the new building being set up?

Audric smiled. "Us and many other hard-working people. Do you have an interest in the Forum?"

"It could be. I already bring over finished pottery, which is sold in Lundenwic, Rochester and Canterbury. I return with lamb's fleeces and leather hides that we buy mainly using coinage obtained for the pottery. That's most of our trade, but we could move much more, particularly high-value items. Trade here has increased dramatically in the last year, and your Forum seems a good idea. I'd like to move a wider range of goods. Despite the demand, there's a limit to the amount of pottery I can sell."

I butted in, "How do you cope with those rough seas? They make me sick just looking at the boats bobbing up and down."

"You're not a seaman then? Even some seasoned seamen suffer seasickness, but you learn to live with it. You'll both have to come out one day. Sometimes I just go down the coastline and back."

"Aye, maybe, but I can go down the coast on horseback."

"But can you move as many goods with a horse and cart and avoid the tribes who think you're easy pickings?"

I conceded, "You have me there, but it may take me time to get used to the idea."

Audric explained where we lived and suggested he and the boy come over tomorrow at midday as he had some trades he'd like to discuss, and they could have a look around the Forum.

I thought, *'Is Audric finally going to let go of his precious goods?'*

By the time Perron and Gabriel, arrived we had dug up and assembled some of Audric's collection of mainly silverware and glassware, and it looked impressive. Perron looked on and handled some of the items before expressing his admiration for the goods. "You've assembled quite a collection of high-value goods which are distinctive and should fetch good prices with the right people. I can't afford to buy such items myself, but back in France, there are noblemen and wealthy landowners who might bargain generous coinage to own such goods. We have markets like here, but the best prices come from visiting the rich people. With the Forum, you should attract plenty of buyers for your attractive goods, but it's only the last year or so that I have seen items of this quality being traded in Britain. France has more wealthy areas where the goods of this type can be traded, and maybe the same can be said of Germany and Italy where I guess some of the items were made."

Audric pondered a short while. "At the moment, there are not sufficient goods to justify us travelling overseas, but I agree that there may not be enough demand here to get high coinage. I would like to split the collection and see where the trading proves most beneficial. I'd like to start to bring in goods from overseas, such as some of your pottery. Short term, it may be easier for me to sell pottery here than the silverware.

"What if I exchange half our collection for an agreed range of your pottery? We'll combine the coinage we make and share in the success or failures. Both here and in your homeland, we would each have a wider range of goods to sell. I think our trust in each other exists through your son and the event down on the dock. In the long term, we want to travel overseas, but for now, we need to build up our resources and learn our trade."

Perron was clearly impressed by what Audric had to say. By exchanging goods, the risk was not too great, and the rewards could be high.

"I believe your idea could work well, but let me think about it overnight. Let's meet again down on the boat, and I'll take you both out to sea. How does that sound, Tork? Let's see if we can make a seaman out of you."

"I'll give it a go, but just make sure you get us back to shore," I said, smiling.

At that, we ambled off after agreeing to return the following day.

Audric spent time that evening thinking about the goods he would exchange for pottery and the ones he would sell locally, possibly through the Forum. I spent time worrying about going to sea until Canu found me and started signing. He was enjoying the farm work and living in Lundenwic. There was a lot to see and far more people than he had ever seen before. I tried to explain about going to sea, and I was a bit afraid, but he smiled and pointed away, suggesting he would like to join us. I nodded, and he gave a large grin. He put up his thumb then dashed off, probably to tell his father.

The next morning, the three of us set off on what looked like being a pleasant day, and the river looked calm. Perron and the boy spotted us from the deck and waved. I took a deep breath as we boarded the boat and felt the first roll, gently up and down. I held onto the side of the boat and saw the others smiling at each other.

Perron pointed across the boat, "There is a cabin over there if we need it, but for the moment, we'll stay on deck. Try to avoid looking in the same direction for too long, and if it gets rough, go to the cabin. If you feel seasick, put your head down between your legs, that seems to work for some people. Otherwise, I hope you enjoy the trip."

The boat was pushed away from the side, the sails were pulled into place, and the boat made a sudden lurch forward, taking us by surprise. We caught our balance and held tight to the side of the boat to enjoy the view. We were with the tide and moved along at a good pace.

Audric asked, "How are you feeling, Tork?"

"Fine, so far. I might even enjoy myself."

Canu was thrilled, laughing and pointing at everything he saw. He and the boy quickly made friends, and Gabriel soon understood that Canu was deaf. As I'd done in the past, he began to improvise signs and show how the boat worked.

Perron was steering down the river and chatting with Audric. We made good time down to the estuary as the tidal flow quickened and the wind got stronger. Then the boat was eased over to a more northerly course, and we eventually came ashore at a small port where Perron had business to do. We went on dry land, and Perron told us to take a stroll whilst he concluded a deal. He'd be back mid-afternoon in time to catch the tide back to Lundenwic. The port was very small and seemed to be dealing mainly with grain which was being held in large timber lined bunkers dug into the ground, something we'd never seen before.

As we set off on our return voyage, I felt pleased that I was not being overawed by the boat journey. The tidal water was moving us along at a steady pace, and the wind in my face was refreshingly fun.

Audric and I were joking about my conversion to a sailor when the boat began to lean further to the leeward, and we heard shouting from the men on board. Perron was yelling back at the men, and Audric ran to his side. There was a serious risk the boat would capsize, and in tidal waters, we'd have little chance of survival.

"Your cargo of grain is shifting; a timber shift board has snapped," Audric explained.

Perron immediately turned the wheel so that the sails lost the wind. The boat corrected its lean slightly but was still tilting badly.

"Audric, I need to stay at the wheel. Tell the men what you know, then they'll try to correct the movement of the grain. Help them if you can."

We shuffled precariously along the leaning deck. "Your cargo is shifting!" shouted Audric.

The men knew instantly what to do and jumped down the hatches in the deck. They scrambled over the grain and quickly improvised a timber brace to the opening where the grain was sliding through. We all shovelled the grain like mad to try and counterbalance the boat's lean.

Slowly the boat began to level off, and one of the men yelled, "You, come with me, we need to lower the masts and then drop anchor. The rest of you, carry on shovelling until we have fully righted, then check all the shift boards are secure, and we'll repair the damaged board shortly."

After the initial drama, it didn't take long to repair the shift board, and once Perron had carried out an inspection, we were on our way again as if nothing had happened.

"How did you know so quickly that the cargo was shifting?" Perron asked Audric.

"Like with your boy, I have this sharp sense when there is danger. I heard the creak of timber breaking, and then my body just felt the movement of the cargo below. Seeing some of the grain being loaded when we boarded probably helped me visualise the situation."

"Well, you may have saved us from capsizing the boat, so thank the Lord."

"Aye, you can say that again," I said.

The rest of our return journey was uneventful, and we arrived back in Lundenwic late evening. Audric and Perron had done their business during the trip and reached an agreement on how they would trade and share the coinage when Perron completed his next round journey overseas.

Later Audric explained how things would work, but he knew by now that I trusted in his judgement.

"As long as we have the farm or a roof over our heads, I'm happy," I concluded.

Audric confirmed his plans would take time. "It will be a year or two before we reach a point where we might be ready to travel overseas and undertake our own trading."

The meeting with Perron set in place a new period in Audric's ambitions, and things moved at a great pace in the following year.

Chapter 16

I made a point of speaking with the landowner, Baden, and he agreed that our farmland could be doubled in size, subject to certain conditions. This enabled us to breed more sheep and a few additional cattle to a level that would more fully support Elred and Canu in the future. Baden had also been in favour of the Forum, and so I discussed our plans to trade and received great encouragement. Baden was probably the wealthiest landowner in this part of the kingdom and well-liked by the Mercian King, AEthelred.

Baden had not been aware of my collection of silverware, so he asked to see some of our goods, and within a few days, we had our first trades. The coinage received was very generous, but Baden thought it warranted for items of such good quality. He was always on the lookout for silverware that might impress other landowners and visiting church superiors.

Before his journey back to France, Perron packed and stored the goods agreed, and we unloaded several crates of fine pottery, checking carefully for breakages. We soon realised that they were well packed, which was very encouraging as we still had to get them back to the farm in one piece.

"This is a good start," Tork said. "When will the Forum open?"

"Yes, we've been fortunate so far. I'm hoping we can have the building all set up next week and have an auction the following Wednesday. There may be a lot of local interest, but it could take some time before those who have the coinage learn of the Forum and make their presence felt."

"Aye, and we'll have to watch out for those who think they can have the goods for nothing. If they didn't know of our haul of silverware, they soon will."

"I'm hoping that our collective of traders provides some form of protection. I don't want to use too many guards, but we may need to keep a keen eye on things."

"Your deal with Baden leaves us holding a lot of coinage. Will that be safe?"

"We'll use much of it to buy extra sheep and further goods. Wool prices seem to be soaring. Baden raised the same issue with me and said he will hold the coinage in a secure place if we wish."

"In the meantime, I'll sleep near our pots of treasure and dream of going to France one day."

"Ah, so you have taken a liking to the sea?"

"Aye, despite the boat nearly capsizing, I really enjoyed being on the boat, away from the bustle of town."

It took a few days of hard work to get the Forum fitted out and for those tasked with running the place to understand their roles. The first day was an opening event when people could come along and view the goods on offer prior to the auction. Each trader had a designated seal, and their items were numbered. Potential buyers had to pay for the goods immediately or agree with the trader on other terms of trade. The crowds flocked to the building, but we had people on the door using their discretion to discourage too many casual lookers. Traders stood by their stands and talked about the goods on display with great interest, though we guessed that many would not have the resources to buy such items.

Our stand was one of the smaller ones, and we had ten pieces of silverware all shined to attract attention and accentuate their beauty. Next to our stand was the leather goods maker, Arrandi, who had made our new boots and treated us kindly during our time in Lundenwic. Beyond him, we could see some marvellous glassware of different colours and shapes; much we had never seen before, suggesting the Forum had attracted new traders. We had an additional stand for Perron's pottery which looked splendid with its array of mugs, vases and plates with a high-quality finish and lovely emboldened patterns. There were several displays of jewellery, from brightly coloured beads to silver and gold rings and bracelets. Rolls of beautiful silk and linen were on show that only the wealthy merchants or landowners could buy. Furs and horns were prominent and would attract the elite members of the local tribes who wanted to look distinctive in their warlike garments. Amongst all these stands were many unusual pieces of little practical use brought from different parts of the world but presumably of ornamental interest to the buyers. Word of mouth had attracted many merchants that we had not seen before, some having come in by boat in the last few days. Several were of foreign appearance and wore well-made, colourful garments. Overall, the signs were very good for our first sale tomorrow.

The day of the auction arrived with great excitement, the buyers standing at the doors and a large crowd of people hanging around to enjoy the atmosphere. The first auctioneer was soon in action, having transferred his skills from selling sheep fleeces to more exotic goods. He rattled through one deal after another, and the bids came in thick and fast. After a long stint at the lectern, a fellow auctioneer took up the reins, and the bidding continued at a pace. There were multiple bidders on nearly every item, and the buyers had come with a clear purpose, to buy.

Come midday, the majority of goods had been sold with just a few items not receiving acceptable bids and remaining with the traders. The auction proved more exciting than I ever expected and there was added excitement as each of our pieces of silverware were sold to the highest bidder. Some merchants made many bids, and one took most of the pottery belonging to Perron. The buying had been fever pitch, despite the number of genuine buyers being less than a hundred.

By late afternoon, the stands were clear; the buyers had disappeared as fast as they had made their bids, and the unsold pieces were packed away by the traders. A few of them remained and were enjoying each other's company over a keg of wine. The Forum had been a great success, and the message would spread, bringing in new traders.

"We've had a wonderful day," Tork shouted across to me. "I never imagined it would be so exciting."

"It does get the blood flowing at a good pace," I responded with a grin on my face. "It's a long way from our work on the farm. Let's join the others for a drink."

"Aye, I'm dying of thirst. I barely thought about food or drink during all the activity. We must be heading for more coinage than we have ever held in our lives."

"You're probably right, but I see it as a measure of our success rather than our wealth. Now let's get that drink."

As we crossed the floor of the Forum, Claude looked our way. "Come and enjoy our celebration. It's been an unbelievable day. Did you ever imagine it would be so successful?"

I looked on proudly but offered a word of caution. "This is just the first day, and clearly, the word got about during all the building work, but we can't be sure the level of activity will be maintained in the long term."

"I'd be surprised if it didn't get even busier," replied Claude.

The others broke in with similar comments and poured us a large share of wine before breaking into local seafaring songs. The group got bigger and noisier as the wine went down. We set off back to the farm with an empty cart and our heads spinning from the drink.

"I'm not sure all that drink was a good idea and carrying this amount of coinage," Tork queried.

"Ah, don't worry, we're only a short distance from the farm," I answered, my body enjoying the effect of the wine. I momentarily reflected that maybe we had become a little too complacent, and sure enough, it didn't take too long for our position to look precarious. We came off the road and headed down the track to the farm with the sun almost down and darkness descending. Out from the wood came six armed men, with one restraining a fierce-looking dog. Our horse lurched forward, lost its footing, and tipped the cart and both of us onto the ground. The men started to laugh and surrounded us in a very menacing way, knives at the ready. Tork looked at me, expecting a response, but I was worse for the fall and maybe the drink.

He was about to draw his knife when I squirmed, "No, we are beaten on this occasion; drop your knife."

Tork let out a "But!" as I cut him short again.

"Do as I say, Tork."

The man with the dog laughed again and picked up our coinage bag lying by my side. "By God, that was easier than I expected. Now bugger off before we slit your throats."

Tork was fuming and ready to fight, but I stood up and dragged him upright.

"Let's go, what we made once we can make again. It's not worth fighting over."

We set off down the track with just a short distance to go to the farm buildings when I said, "Get ready to run when you hear them shout. Then, if they come for us, are you up for teaching them a lesson or two?"

"Aye, that's more like it."

It didn't take long before the shouting began, and they were chasing after us, dropping our bag of coinage. They released the dog, which came charging at us with 'kill' written in its eyes, but before it reached us, it slowed down and meekly sidled alongside. I ruffled its ears and spoke gently to the dog, which then turned and set off towards the gang of men.

"Sher", I commanded.

Out of the trees, the magnificent Sher swooped down on the men causing two to fall over. The dog's owner screamed as his dog jumped at him, fiercely gripping the man's arm. Two men turned and fled away, leaving one man standing, frightened to move. We charged at them, ready to fight, if necessary, but they jumped up and ran off with the dog growling to help them on their way. Sher shrieked and swooped to add to their dismay, and we laughed at the sight of them being chased off by their own dog.

Tork bent down to retrieve the bag of coins, "Thank goodness we got this back."

I couldn't help but give a cheeky smile. "You can leave that there; it's just a bag of pebbles."

Tork opened the bag and then roared with laughter. "I should have guessed you wouldn't give up your fortune so easily, but when did you make the switch?"

"I believe it was before we started drinking, my dear Tork. It's in the secure possession of Baden and his guards, as is the coinage of several other traders. An agreement was made some time ago, but it was important that no word got out and that we held onto the bag as if our lives depended on it."

"Well, it was a bit of a scare, but the sight of those rogues being chased off by their own dog made it all worthwhile."

"I don't expect them back, but Sher will watch them over the next few days."

As we approached the farm buildings, there was a bark from behind us.

Tork turned to see the dog again and reached for his knife, but I said, "No need; Star, come here, boy."

He came up to us in a meek but cheerful manner and licked my hand.

Tork patted the dog, which seemed a different animal to the one set on us earlier. "We seem to have made a new friend, but he could be a fierce beast amongst our livestock."

"I think he has been badly treated and just needs good care and a little further training. He will make a fine guard dog for Elred and Canu whilst we are away."

"He certainly frightened me to death. I was ready to use my knife until you calmed him with your ways."

"I've shaken off the drink after that escapade, but let's get inside and rest up."

It was a calm night, and the dog remained peaceful until morning when he made a slight yelp, and I awoke to see him licking Tork's face. Star was looking at Tork expectantly, and I guessed he needed food or a walk outside. Tork led him out on a length of rope to be sure he wasn't about to run after the sheep. I followed them out as Star was walked to the fencing and eased back when he seemed inclined to head for the livestock. Tork left him tied to the fencing so the animals could get used to each other and gave him food and water.

Amazingly, two of the sheep came up to the fence approaching without fear, and the dog remained calm. I am sure Tork was wondering if this was the same animal that looked as though it would rip out our throats as he took off Star's lead and let him roam, but the dog remained settled and made no attempt to chase the sheep.

I wandered over to join them. "I see you have completed Star's training in no time at all. Well done. You'll soon have a friend for life."

"Aye, it's amazing how quickly they grow on you. Your manner with the dog yesterday has changed him beyond recognition."

"They have to want to change, and Star is one of those animals who deserve a better master."

Soon Elred and Canu came out of their dwelling, and Star began running back and forth between us all with great excitement. We explained what had happened, and Elred was delighted to have the dog on the farm.

Before long, Canu and Tork had built a small hut for our new friend, and he responded well to our calls. Even Canu taught Star to come to him on the sound of a quick clap of hands.

For the next few days, the dog was the centre of attention, and you couldn't ignore him, but he gradually settled and learned to spend time on his own.

Routine on the farm was restored, and we could see the land was in good hands as Elred and Canu only needed occasional help, so we turned our attention back to planning the next stage of our trading.

Chapter 17

At the auction, we not only sold all our silverware and some glassware, but we also bought several items of silk and well-produced linen. I talked about how we needed to replenish our stocks from more sources than just the local market. We would need to build up good relations with all the traders, merchants and wealthy private buyers. In some ways, this was no different to the trading of our sheep fleeces, but the range of goods made it far more complicated.

I suggested that now might be the time to use our coinage to buy the land where we farmed. The risk of losing the large amount of accumulated wealth would then be Baden's responsibility, and he had the men and buildings to secure such riches.

"We would be landowners?" Tork exclaimed. "But what if we left to travel?"

"We would still be the landowners when we returned," I answered, "and Elred would manage the farm in our absence."

"I still think of myself as a peasant farmer. Things have changed in the last few years."

"There is nothing wrong with being a farm labourer and making a living from the land. We are doing that successfully and have every right to own a plot of land, provided the landowner will sell it to us. One day, Baden may not be here, and without the ownership of the land, we could be thrown off the farm despite all the hard work we've put in."

"Aye, I'd hate that to happen after all the work we've done. Let's see if Baden is prepared to sell."

Our talks with Baden went well, and he was delighted with the idea. He always needed coinage to maintain his buildings to a high standard and keep men to protect his land. He feared more invasions, and the Mercians may not always be around to defend them. Raising an army always required coinage if mercenaries were needed to back up the local tribes.

A deal was struck, and we were now the owners of our farm and the land it stood upon. We decided to call it Morland after my former master, Morgan. Tork created a timber plaque, inscribed the name with his knife and hung it from a tree near the entrance to the farm track. It was a proud moment to own the land beneath our feet, and it was a very comforting feeling.

"Does this mean we won't be going to sea anytime soon?" Tork queried.

"There's still much to do and learn here in Britain, and Morland will be a wonderful place to return to as we come back from our travels. In fact, I want us to return to Rochester to see how the people there are getting on and if we can help in any way. In addition, we can check the trading conditions there and see if Abbot Wilfrid got off safely to Rome."

"I can't imagine how far that must be and the toll it must take on the body. The abbot is a very determined man but no spring chicken."

"He'll have a good escort, and many churches and monasteries will put him up each night. That's one advantage of being part of a religious order. Also, the weather is warmer further south, and after our recent winters, I'm sure he'll be glad to be in Rome."

"Aye, I wouldn't mind some of that warmth myself. Those deep frosts we had last winter went straight through me."

"It won't be long, another year or two, then we'll set sail to other lands. For the moment, we wait for Perron to return and listen to his stories."

"When do you expect him back?"

"In a few more weeks. He needs time to sell the goods he has taken back and stock up with new pottery and maybe a few other types of goods I asked him to look out for. We need to buy new goods, and I'm hoping Rochester or Canterbury will provide them. Let's tell Elred our plans and get ready to set off tomorrow."

Signs of autumn were in the air when we rode out the following morning, the wind blowing from the west and leaves starting to fall from the trees. Star made to follow us, but my firm command sent him scurrying back to Canu, who was waving us off. That evening we camped short of Rochester, so we could enter early morning and assess the extent of the recovery from the devastation caused by the Mercians. I prompted Tork to talk more of Morgan and their times together.

Wine in hand, around the campfire, Tork talked of the time he and Morgan had got embroiled with warring factions.

"The attack you and I experienced in Eoforwic was not the first time the Mercians tried to take land in Northumbria. Wulfhere's father, Penda, made a similar attempt about two decades ago. He had a large army with many overlords and besieged Oswiu and his men in the north of Northumbria, taking Oswiu's son hostage. You can now see similarities with what happened in Eoforwic. Anyway, Oswiu paid a large amount of treasure to Penda to depart the siege and release his son. Penda then set off back to Mercia, claiming a great victory, but Oswiu could not contain his anger and set off in pursuit of the Mercian army.

"Unfortunately, we were out on our travels at the time, and despite attempts to evade the Mercian army, we followed a track to a small clearing and headed straight into the midst of a group of warriors. They quickly corralled us, and whilst Master gave them a plausible explanation for our movements, we were forced to ride with them back to Penda's army. By now, we realised that the Northumbrians, under Oswiu, must be in pursuit of Penda. Morgan restated that we were not men of war, but the king himself said we could choose the sword now or fight with his men. Our choice was to die now or risk being killed in action against the Northumbrians to whom we had a greater allegiance. Master played for time, and we fell in line with the Mercians. By the time the sun was high in the sky, the two armies were gazing at each other across a deep valley with the Northumbrians stretched out along a high ridge, looking all the more dominant force.

"Before we had a chance to retreat and hide away, the war cries had begun, and we were heading into battle. In our first confrontation, we only had knives to hand, but we unsaddled two riders and gained their shields and spears. Next, Master brought several riders to the ground in ways I didn't understand, and we rode through the melee. Then our shields dispatched more riders from their horses, and suddenly, there seemed to be a gap in the Northumbrian lines.

"I remember Master shouting, "Ride like the wind," and somehow, our horses took us well away from danger. We reined in the horses in a secluded location to catch our breath, but the crashing of shields and shrieks of pain still rang in our ears.

"A few days later, we came back that way, and the death toll was evidence of a brutal battle. There, in the middle of the battlefield, was a large stake in the ground, topped with a warrior's head, blood-stained and its eyes glazed with horror. That was Penda's last battle.

"Twenty years on, as you know, Wulfhere endeavoured to change that when he passed through Elmet and came on to Eoforwic looking to avenge his father's death. Your efforts prevented a massacre like the one Master and I escaped."

I looked at Tork thoughtfully, "As a young boy, I could never understand why the warriors attacked our farmland and destroyed our community and today, I still don't comprehend what happened. We live in fear of the next invasion, and Morland could be lost just as Rochester has been ravaged."

"Aye, and yet life goes on. People don't seem to give in. Remember how when we left Rochester the last time, everyone was helping each other to recover."

"Let's hope we see more of that tomorrow," I sighed.

I woke the following morning to find Tork up and about and looking eager to get underway.

The birds were chirping, and the morning mist was clearing as the sun came up. The promise of a fine day was welcome after our sombre conversation last night. We rode down into Rochester and realised it must be market day as stallholders were setting up for the day. It was quiet, but there was a degree of cheerfulness around, and repairs had been carried out on many buildings previously in partial ruin. Progress was good, but there was still evidence of the aftermath of the rampage carried out by the Mercian army. Outwardly things seemed to be going in the right direction, but behind closed doors, the torment would still be raw.

We soon came across some of the men we had worked with before, and we received nods of welcome. We had no firm plans of where we would stay and were not inclined to approach the church on this visit. On dismounting in the market square, two of the men approached us that we recognised as Utred and Alcin, market traders.

"Welcome back," said Utred. "We didn't expect you back so soon. You both look well. How can we help you, or are you here to give us more support? We have not forgotten the help you gave us in very difficult times when we were still mourning our losses. We continue to mourn, but the thoughts have lightened."

I shook their hands. "Time is a great healer, but we understand that you continue to miss your loved ones and friends you lost. We will help where we can and look forward to meeting more of the townsfolk. Is there anywhere we can stay for a while?"

Alcin smiled, "I've got plenty of space, and you're welcome to use it as long as you wish. When you're ready, I'll take you there."

"Thanks," I replied. "We'll come back later when the market closes."

Emotionally, those who had survived the attack seemed much better and ready to get on with life the best they could. The farms had organised the labour to good effect and kept supplies of food going out to the people, so there were no signs of starvation. Where there were problems, we made a mental note to see what help could be provided. This involved mainly young women with children without their husbands, killed by the Mercians.

We called back at the market and found food and drink available, which sustained us through the afternoon whilst we made more enquiries. What was obvious was the need for more menfolk and more families to move to Rochester: not something that could be readily organised. There would be a stigma about the town for years to come unless the traders could make the town increasingly attractive.

I suggested a meeting of the men charged with organising the town's recovery. Over the next few days, we made contact with the two main landowners and the church that controlled most of the land. I persuaded them that they needed to attract more people to Rochester, and it was in their interest to make land available to create more wealth for the town. Working with the townsfolk, additional dwellings should be erected to induce people to settle in Rochester. Simple improvements to the riverside would allow bigger boats to come alongside to load and unload goods. Some of the traders should come up to Lundenwic and see what is happening there. Similarly, crop growing might be done on a larger scale to feed the townsfolk, landowners and church brethren. Subject to making good use of the land, the tenants should have a right to buy the land at a fair price after five years. All these inducements would reach people by word of mouth, and soon, Rochester should be thriving.

We continued in this vein day after day and provided greater detail as required.

"Enthusiasm seems high," said Tork, "and you've got them well organised."

"I think so. It's probably time for us to return to Morland; they'll be wondering where we've got to," I replied.

We had done our bit and worked pretty hard, physically and mentally, to get things moving.

"I'd like to talk to some of the leaders before we return."

"They'll want you to stay," Tork suggested.

"I think they have their own leaders now, and we are not far away if needed."

Many locals gathered to listen as I announced our farewell.

"You have gone through terrible times, and for many of you, there is still grieving to be done, but you have made tremendous progress to get the town back on its feet. Your leaders are well organised and should guide you well in the future. You are welcome to Lundenwic any time if you need help, and we would like to thank you for your wonderful kindness whilst we have been staying here."

Our host, whilst in Rochester, Alcin, stepped forward. "We have so much to thank these two great men who have shared our adversity and worked long hours to support us. In addition, they have become wonderful friends to the community and let's hope it is not the last time we see them. Give them a rousing farewell."

A loud roar arose, and people came forward to shake our hands and pat us on the back. It was an emotional moment, and the feeling lingered as we walked back to Alcin's dwelling.

In the early morning, we headed back to Morland as the trees were rapidly losing their leaves, and the hue of colours was disappearing. As we reached home, Star raced down the track with great excitement, and Canu was not far behind. After a long ride, we were ready to dismount and jumped down to greet them both. I was still amazed at the friendly, good nature of Star compared with our first confrontation. He ran between us both in a short frenzy before settling down and walking alongside us back to the farm buildings where Elred stood waiting. Canu was busy signing to Tork, and I sensed that he had missed us and was worried that we were not returning.

Elred told us Perron had arrived back a few days ago and was hoping to catch up with us shortly. The farm was running smoothly, and though he'd not been to the Forum since we were last here, it seems that it had been busy. He and Canu were well, and he expressed his thanks again for allowing them the opportunity to run the farm.

"I'm not sure where we would have ended up if we hadn't met you," said Elred. "We weren't planning to go back to farming, but I think our time here shows that it's for the best. The loss of my wife, Faith, made me think I needed a change, but it was more that I needed time to get over her death."

I looked on with sympathy. "It's worked out well for all of us, and you can stay as long as you wish. One day I hope we can pass the farm on to you and Canu."

Elred looked emotional and didn't speak, but Tork announced, "Audric has new plans by the day, so who knows where we'll be next year, but it will always be good to come back to Morland

and see you both - and Star, of course. How's he coping with the livestock?"

Elred seemed cheered, "He's fine. He seems to have this knack of acting like one of them. He's not trained to round up sheep, but he does sense when we need support and will help with any strays. Canu loves him, and they often go for a walk together. Strangely the dog doesn't even chase the foxes or wild boars unless they come near the livestock."

Canu smiled and gave the dog a friendly stroke. Star looked around at us all and wagged his tail as if to join in the talk, and suddenly Sher swooped in with a squawk to remind us he was still here. I looked around as a tear came to my eye as I thought of the family we'd returned to, and I reflected on my lost parents.

Chapter 18

We wasted no time catching up with Perron, and it was good to see young Gabriel looking fit and well. Perron's journey back to France had been successful. He had sold our silverware at a very good price, and there was a demand for more pieces of that quality. He had returned with some more pottery and beautiful glassware containing swirls of colour and an array of different shapes. He also had a small bag of glass beaded necklaces of a very original design that he felt would sell well here. Perron and I compared the trades we had both achieved and came to an adjustment of the coinage that suited us both. There was nothing to send back to France this time, but I agreed to take all Perron's stock to the next trading day at the Forum and would start building up more silverware from markets in Lundenwic, Rochester and Canterbury.

More and more people were making Lundenwic their place to live, and working conditions were becoming cramped and dirty. I talked to many traders and new arrivals about better opportunities in Rochester, and some seemed to take my advice when seeing the congestion in Lundenwic. A lot of waste was being dumped in the river, and only the strong tidal flows stopped it from festering on the shorelines.

Back at the farm, the air was fresh, and the contrast with the town centre was becoming very noticeable.

"There's something to be said for life on the farm," said Tork, taking a deep breath.

"The situation is getting worse as more people arrive," I confirmed. "We'll soon need better planning to handle all the changes taking place and have enough clean water available. We can take cleaner water from upriver, but many take it out locally when the wells run dry and risk fever or stomach cramps."

"We'll all have to change our ways in time or suffer the consequences. They say the Romans used to run canals to route water from the river into the towns. There are still remains of the stone channels they built inside the walls, and then the water was stored underground to be pumped up later."

"As you say, Tork, and yet hundreds of years later, we're no further forward; in fact, we've gone backwards. That's one good reason to travel and see what other countries are doing. It's not just trading exotic goods but how they run their large towns and farms. We're a peasant society stuck in time. Why do we have so few stone buildings that will survive like those the Romans built?"

"Aye, I understand, but come on; don't get too low. You've done so much to help the communities here and in Rochester."

"Thanks, you have a good knack of keeping my spirits up."

We spent more time on the farm after our weeks away, perhaps to avoid some of the ugly aspects of the town. We were preparing for another hard winter, and that's exactly what we got. Everything ground to a halt, and it became a matter of survival once more as we entered day after day of hard frost. The land was rock hard, and icicles hung from the trees, with just a few drops of water following the occasional midday sunshine. The Thames was totally frozen and the ice thick enough that people were wandering back and forth without concern. Children were playing games on the ice, and a few traders set up hot food stalls.

Pagan or Christian in origin, the people looked forward to the mass winter festival of food and drink, largely subsidised by the landowners. On the day, it was a colourful spectacle with stalls and bunting alongside Baden's home. Plenty of fire pits and a central bonfire provided some warmth as people circulated and gorged on food and drank copious amounts of mead, cider, beer and wine. As the day progressed, groups congregated and began to sing and dance, and we joined in the merriment. Canu was dancing in a circle, and Star ran around him as if to copy his movement. A pleasant, middle-aged lady was dancing and chatting with Elred, which brought a smile to my face, and I hoped that they would make good company for each other. I couldn't remember the last time I had enjoyed myself so much, dancing, laughing and singing away. Tork gave the dancing and singing a good go. At one point, Canu grabbed him, and they swung each other around before falling over in a heap and laughing loudly, Star looking on with a bemused expression. The evening light faded, and the townsfolk drifted home as the severe cold descended. Another year had gone by, and barely five years since I first met Tork.

Warmer weather brought a gradual thaw, and it was dramatic to watch the ice over the river break apart in large sections with the occasional warning sign from deep sounding cracking noises. The land remained rock hard for some time, but the sheep were turned out onto the pastures to graze. The lambing season was soon upon us, and spring lightened our spirits once again.

It was over a year since my last alter ego dream, but I was not to be spared despite the joys of spring. I often daydreamed of the future, but that night, the intruder arrived in his usual antagonistic way.

"You're idling your time away, looking after peasants in Rochester and Lundenwic."

"They need help more than most," I countered.

"And why waste your time on buying and selling trinkets?"

"*Because the 'trinkets,' as you call them, reflect more advanced societies that can lead us to a better way of life.*"

"*You even interfere with the ways of the church, through Abbot Wilfrid, but you don't believe in God.*"

"*It's important to deal with all people in a compassionate way, whatever their beliefs.*"

"*You don't treat me with compassion.*"

"*Maybe you don't deserve it.*"

"*Have you found your parents yet?*"

"*You know they are probably dead after all this time.*"

"*That's not what I think.*"

"*What makes you say that?*"

"*You're not the only one who has premonitions.*"

"*Tell me what you mean. I don't trust you.*"

"*Then there is no point in telling you my secret.*"

"*Secret? You have no meaningful secrets.*"

"*Follow me into battle, and I will lead you to our parents.*"

"*They are not your parents! You'll lead me nowhere. But what do you know about my parent's existence?*"

"*So, you are interested?*"

"*Maybe.*"

"*Then I'll be blunt. Return to Ripon. The Mercians are to attack Northumbria again. This time you'll fight for the Northumbria cause and show your worth.*"

"*And if I agree, you'll tell me where my parents are?*"

"*Yes, that will be the easy part.*"

"*I'll think about it.*"

"*Unless you take action, this is the last time you'll hear from me.*"

The remainder of the night, my sleep was erratic, and thoughts passed in great swathes of emotions until I woke, exhausted. Despite great tiredness, my mind was resolved. I would return to Ripon and try to contact Aldren or Oldred.

Before that, I needed to ensure the Forum was working well and our trading efforts continued to be successful. With spring underway, the markets became busy, and the first opening of the year for the Forum was planned for the following week. Traders and merchants had provided some of their goods for display and requested stalls for auction day. The quality of the goods throughout the Forum building was better than ever, suggesting the traders and merchants were very confident of selling their items. The number of boats offshore increased daily, and Perron's boat came into view the day before the auction. We worked hard to offload his goods and took these to the Forum.

The first auction of the year was a great success. People came from all directions with their horses and carts, and boats were spread all along the shoreline. Food stalls did a roaring trade, and beer and wine were flowing from casks set up alongside improvised tables and chairs. The traditional fleece sales thrived adjacent to the Forum, and trades were fetching the best prices in years.

I was also relieved to hear that the Mercians had largely withdrawn their presence in Rochester, and the local noblemen were re-establishing their dominance. AEthelred was apparently more concerned with achieving control of Northumbria after the Mercians' embarrassing failure under his brother Wulfhere. Particularly for the people of Rochester, this offered great relief and enabled them to contemplate a secure future.

Back at Morland, the ewes had lambed, and the fields were a joyful scene of greenery and new life. More exciting was the news that Elred and Meru were to marry, and she would come and live on the farm. We were becoming quite wealthy and could soon consider travelling overseas and operating in the ways of a merchant. I suggested to Tork that spring next year would be the best time to set off and maybe travel initially with Perron to use his experience.

"In the meantime, Tork, I need to return to Ripon. A short while ago, I had a premonition and, since then, a recurring dream. I find it difficult to talk about the nature of the vision, but the essence is that the Mercians are planning a further attack on Northumbria. Plus, more importantly to me, if I help the Northumbrians, it will lead to the discovery of my parent's whereabouts."

"Can you trust a dream? Getting involved in war again seems to conflict with your ideology, though I understand you want to find out what has happened to your parents."

"I can't think beyond my parents at the moment. You don't need to be involved."

"Aye, that's true, but you may need my help, and it should be a nostalgic return."

"Remember, I'm going to aid the Northumbrians, which could lead us to war."

"We'll take it a step at a time. When do you want to leave?"

"A couple of days' time when we've told people our plans."

"I'll sort out the travel packs. I assume we just want our horses and a packhorse and to travel light."

"That's fine, no carts, no goods and no trading on this trip. Thank you, Tork; I'll never forget the support you give me."

Chapter 19

I hadn't imagined that we would be retracing our steps anytime soon, but here we were, heading north, joining one of the main Roman roads, appearing worse for wear than on our journey south from Eoforwic to Lundenwic. There were many more people travelling south than in our direction, confirming what we already knew - that word of mouth was telling them that there were increasing opportunities to be had in the Angles regions. Our plan was to go via Eoforwic and on to Ripon and hope to avoid the type of trouble we had experienced before. The late summer weather was kind, and our aim was to camp unless the rains came, and then we would seek shelter.

Day after day, we made good progress, occasionally stopping to talk with travellers and pick up gossip. Small numbers of tribal warriors had been seen but nothing leading to trouble, and as yet, there was no talk of war. We passed through Elmet and rode on towards Tadcaster, remembering the events of the past. The final stretch of the road into Eoforwic was busy, and we realised it must be a market day. We entered the same gate that the Mercians had passed through when they were corralled and taken prisoner. That had worked out well in contrast to the devastation caused in Rochester by the Mercian army. There was a lot of activity in the market, and it was good to see a few food stalls. We'd not eaten much for the last couple of days, so we headed straight over and bought a bowl of stew. Once our appetite had been satisfied, it didn't take long to find the bunkhouse we'd stayed in before, and we took a couple of rooms.

"Let's wander around the market," I suggested, "and see if the town has changed much."

"Aye, I'll be glad to be out of the saddle for a day or two if that's the plan. Do you want to see if the new bishop's in place, and would he want to be bothered with us?"

"We'll make discrete enquiries, and maybe someone will talk to us. You know I'm not the religious type, but I am curious to know what has happened to Abbot Wilfrid's See."

"I wonder if the abbot is in Rome and seen the pope yet. I don't understand how one person can have so much influence on what goes on in another country."

"Well, with Abbot Wilfrid ousted from his position, you can see that the pope doesn't always get his way. Sometimes the nobility ignore his dictates and do whatever suits them. It seems to take the fear of God before they accept the rule from Rome."

"Archbishop Theodore seems to be the one with the most control, even though he showed some sympathy towards Abbot Wilfrid."

"He was sent from Rome, by the pope, to bring the churches in England into some sort of unity, and Abbot Wilfrid was the first casualty of his reforms. He seems a good man and should do well. Let's head to the market and get a bit more food and drink."

We passed the ecclesiastical library, where I had been absorbed by the manuscripts and first realised that I could read Latin fluently. Two monks confirmed no one had yet been appointed to Abbot Wilfrid's position and various understudies were in place at different Sees. The thought was that this might continue for some time. There was still concern about his removal from the position, but they agreed it was unlikely to be rescinded until he came back from Rome, and this could be a year or two. I took the opportunity to look at some of the scripts and soon became lost in a sea of new knowledge whilst Tork said he would sit on the library steps to enjoy the sunshine.

A short while later, I came out into the bright glare of the sun only to find Tork had probably gone for a walk, so I sat down enjoying the warmth of the day. As time passed, I sensed there was a problem, so I allowed my mind to drift until, for a brief moment, I visualised Tork being manhandled by three men, one with a knife to his back. They had headed to a nearby side street where I hurried to see if I could catch sight of them, but the byway was deserted. Continuing down the street, it was like my childhood game of hide and seek on the farm. As I progressed, my heart beat stronger, and I could sense they were all close by. I tried to visualise their whereabouts without success, but my blood was pumping hard, sweat pouring off my brow. Then I picked up talking the other side of a doorway and stood close.

"He'll fetch a good price," someone proffered.

"Yah, not just as a slave on the boats but yar hear of them circus freaks who people pay to see."

I opened the door slightly, and whilst Tork was bound tight, he was not in immediate danger, so I slowly entered the room. "The only freaks I can see are you three goons."

The men turned and pulled out their knives but edged backwards, uncertain what to expect.

I looked deeply into the eyes of the nearest threat, and after a moment, he turned and cut the bands holding Tork. The other men were looking threatening as Tork moved alongside me, and one of them suddenly plunged forward with his knife only to stumble headfirst, short of his target. Now all the men seemed confused. They made a dash for the doorway, but the door slammed shut, and they crashed into each other.

"So, what shall we do with them, Tork?"

By now, Tork had a knife in his hand and was looking at his assailants menacingly. His idea was excellent.

A short while later, all three men were standing stark naked, bound together around a post on the library steps. The gathering crowd were laughing at the men's embarrassment as we stood a short distance away, contemplating our departure.

"Hopefully, they will think twice before attempting that again," Tork said.

Apart from the pleasant atmosphere around Eoforwic, there seemed little to hold us here. Further enquiries revealed that Ecgfrith, the Northumbrian king, tended to remain much further north near the coastal town of Alnwick. However, the overlords, Aldren and Oldred, were often seen around Ripon and occasionally in Eoforwic. They travel with a small force of about a hundred men but only interfere with local affairs if an edict comes from the king. I realised they would be keen to hear my news, but would they believe me?

"I can see you are tense," queried Tork. "You're usually calm, even in difficult times. It won't be long before we reach Ripon, and hopefully, things will start to take shape in the way you want."

"It's certainly taken my attention away from our plans to travel overseas, and yet that's been my aim for the last year or two."

"Aye, you've been one-tracked for a while; you even ignored those beautiful girls at the winter festival that kept asking you to dance."

"Well, not entirely, but it might take a special woman to turn my head."

"Now you're being fussy, or have you met someone whilst my head has been turned?"

"No, you have an eagle eye to match Sher, and you'll probably know before I do."

Tork laughed, "Maybe so!"

"Thanks, Tork; I needed to break out of my thoughts. Let's camp up for the night before going into Ripon. We'll have a drink. and you can tell me more stories about Morgan."

The evening air was cool, so we set up a campfire, ate our pack of food and indulged in a flagon of wine.

"What were your worst moments with your master?" I prompted Tork in our evening conversation.

"That was when the Black Plague was at its worst about ten years ago. Hundreds of people were dying in the surrounding villages, and occasionally entire families were wiped out within a week or two. Master was known for his medicinal potions, so people were constantly knocking on our door to my great concern, but Master turned no one away, providing advice or treatment. He explained to them he could not cure the plague, but what he gave them might help those whose bodies were strong enough to fight the fever. As you can imagine, some people did survive, which only increased Master's reputation as a healer.

"At one point, I was remarking how lucky we were not to go down with the plague. I had tempted fate, and it bit back! Master went into a fever for three days, and I used all the remedies he had been handing out. I was waiting for him to die and me to go down with the illness, but fortunately, neither occurred. Master made a miraculous recovery, and I was lucky not to be struck down. At times it felt worse than war; there was no real way to stop its progress, from person to person and then village to village. The mourning was horrific for both young and old, and no one dared go near anyone who had the plague."

I extended an arm of comfort. "You must have been so afraid at the time."

"When I see bad things happen, I remind myself how lucky we were to survive. In the end, Master did not live many more years after that, but at least he chose his time and place to go. I also believe he was waiting for you to arrive, but I didn't know that when you first appeared at our door."

"That was a strange time. Even though I found Morgan mesmerising, I never imagined what was to follow."

"Aye, you and me both. I can imagine your worst moment was the loss of your parents, but you must have had many good times together?"

"When I was a young boy, maybe five or six, my father used to teach me to ride bareback on a pony. Within a year or so, I was riding confidently, and we were able to go off together into the hills, occasionally hunting for wild boar. He taught me to fish and work on the farm, so by the time I was ten, I had mastered many skills. I still lacked the physical strength needed but could join in most activities. It made me feel like a young man rather than a boy, and I was proud of my part in the family. When we got back from our toiling on the farm, my mother was always there with hot food and a joyful greeting. It was a hard life, particularly when we were on the road, not knowing where the next farm would take us on. We might have been poor, but our collective spirit was always strong. Whilst I had no idea I would meet Morgan, it seemed to be in my mind that one day I would move into a new world of opportunity. However, losing my family at such a young age is my eternal regret."

We consoled ourselves with the wine and spoke of more recent events before turning to sleep under the stars.

By morning, there was a cold chill in the air which encouraged us to rise early and prepare to head off to Ripon.

Chapter 20

The rolling terrain as we approached Ripon gave us occasional glimpses of the new church, and it looked majestic against the surrounding forest land. As we dropped amongst the trees, we lost sight of it again until we reached the outskirts of the town, where the church reappeared in all its glory. The majority of the stone walls were in place, but there was no grand spire yet, though it was easy to imagine how it would dominate the town in the years ahead. Several pulley systems were in use, and the site was very busy, particularly with men shaping the huge joists required for the roof.

It was still early morning and the main street was relatively quiet, so we rode through to the church to see if we could recognise any old friends. We asked after Angus to be told he would return tomorrow. He was now responsible for supervising the work at Hexham as well as Ripon. Apparently, the church in Hexham was nearly finished, with just the interior to complete. We explained our previous involvement and asked if there was still accommodation available for a few nights. A name was provided to follow up later. Further enquiries suggested there was a small tribe of Northumbrian warriors camped a few miles north of the town. The group had been there several days and visited the town to meet landowners or to have a few drinks. They were unsure if any of the overlords were amongst them.

We wove our way back to the workers' bunkhouses where we had stayed before when working in Ripon and secured accommodation for a couple of nights. Having not found anyone we knew well, we set off to the Northumbrian camp. As we approached, there was little to show that this was a warring tribe, apart from several groups of horses being groomed and fed. To avoid anyone getting too excited, we dismounted and walked into the camp. A few early risers watched us cautiously, and finally, two armed warriors approached. We carried daggers readily visible, so we raised our hands slightly to indicate peaceful intent.

I explained, "We are known to your overlords, Aldren and Oldred, and spent time with them when the Mercians attacked Eoforwic a few years ago. We also worked on the construction of the church about the same time."

The more rugged of the two looked at us carefully. "You won't know me, but I remember you both talking to Aldren and Oldred at the time. My understanding is that you helped our cause in sending the Mercians into an ignominious retreat. I guarded over the prisoners at the time, and I remember the dwarf here prowling around. We guessed he was there to ensure we didn't put a few of them to the sword."

"Aye, something like that," Tork whispered.

I intervened, "Are Aldren or Oldred in the camp?

"Not too far away," came the reply. "Can you remind me of your names and wait over by that tent?"

"I'm Audric; this is Tork."

Shortly after, the huge frame of Oldred came bounding towards us, and he put his hands on Tork's shoulders.

"Welcome again, my little friend; we have missed you both, and you, my dear Audric, with the wise head and more a man than ever. What can we do for you? Aldren is away hunting this morning but will be here later, around midday."

I replied, "Best we talk with you both. Shall we call back later?"

"Just after midday should be fine, but what's the mystery?"

"Oh, it's not an immediate problem, so we'll explain it all then. We'll head back to the town until then. It will be good to catch up later."

We spent the rest of the morning wandering around, firstly looking at the progress of the church and then walking around the market seeking food and drink. We met a few people we knew and expressed our admiration over the workmanship on the building. Seeing work on the roof and the spire in progress reminded me of my lucky escape when knocked from my perch on the Hexham church roof.

"Fancy another stint in the rafters?" teased Tork.

"You're not going to let me forget that day, though actually, I loved being up there all alone, looking around the countryside."

"At times, you seem to have no fear."

"Oh, the fear is often there, but you need to keep a clear head when danger comes. I can feel my heart racing, but my mind says control the moment."

"Aye, well, it's worked so far, but let's avoid any risks for now."

Our wander around Ripon was very pleasant. The beautiful surrounding forests had not yet been spoilt by the growth of the town, but it was busy and thriving. There were many more people than on our first visit, and a few workshops had been erected similar to those in Lundenwic. The church was now the dominant feature of the town and probably the driving force behind its growth, as in Eoforwic, Canterbury and Rochester. Our reservations about religion had to be tempered with the way it seemed to hold some communities together. Whilst our journey north took us back in time, the towns were not stuck in a bygone age, and new opportunities were opening up for those who wanted more than to work on the land. This is what was pushing me along a path that one day would see us travelling overseas to explore how other countries lived. However, in the here and now, warring factions were plotting power grabs that could destroy the progress made.

We returned to the Northumbrian campsite to find Aldren had returned with several wild boars in tow, one already being gutted and stripped to cook over the fire pit. We received a cheerful greeting, and he asked if we would join them this evening when a feast was to be held. Clearly, it was going to be a raucous affair, but we felt it important to express our friendship, and so accepted the invitation.

The feast seemed to start well before the evening as wine and cider was soon being consumed in groups around the campsite. We weren't pressed for our news, but I wanted to get over our message before spirits got too out of hand.

"Have you had any trouble since Eoforwic?" I asked.

Aldren smiled, "There have been a few skirmishes on the borders, but I think you have news for us that might change things!"

"It won't be a surprise," I said, "if I tell you that the Mercians are readying to attack Northumbria. We have seen their withdrawal from Rochester and Canterbury and a recent premonition tells me they will move this way soon. We wish to ride with you and fight the Northumbrian cause."

"You seem to have changed your views since we last met. We thought you hated war?"

"I do, but I now realise that sometimes it may be in the interest of the people to defend themselves." *'And I wish to find my parents,'* my thoughts continued.

"Aldren sighed, "We've been expecting an attack ever since we heard of Wulfhere's death and his brother taking the crown."

"My vision only shows the armies confronting each other. I have an idea that could influence the situation."

"And what might that be?" intervened Oldred.

"Northumbria took the Kingdom of Lindsey from the Mercians many years ago, and Mercia have always thought of it as their land. Its position geographically, below the Humber Estuary, will be difficult for you to defend. Your gambit could be to forfeit Lindsey."

Oldred offered his opinion, "If they take Lindsey, they will pause and then come after the rest of the kingdom. Maybe we should make a surprise attack on Mercia."

Aldren filled the void. "Remember, Oldred, we are not the fighting force we were a decade ago, and our king no longer seeks to expand our territory. However, having said that, he does not want to show any weakness that encourages the Mercians to attack.

"You took Lindsey by force," I explained, "simply because the Mercians pushed you back that far when you attacked the whole of Mercia unsuccessfully. They judged at the time it was best to leave Lindsey after a difficult campaign, but historically, it does belong to them. Strategically Lindsey will always be difficult to defend, so why risk losing many men over a kingdom you have only held in recent decades?"

Aldren pondered, "You make it sound so easy, but when two armies face each other, and the blood is boiling, and your cause seems just, it is difficult not to charge into battle. Go give them your advice and let them retreat."

"You have already suggested that your army is not as strong as you would like. This would not be a dishonourable retreat but a sensible withdrawal, with all your force intact, to protect the main part of Northumbria."

"We thank you for your thoughts. The decision will be Ecgfrith's, but even then, I think we will be on the battlefield before the final actions are decided. Your point about not being trapped in Lindsey is well thought out. Do you still intend to stay and fight our cause?"

"Tork and I will remain to fight if needed."

"Then join our evening celebrations," announced Oldred, "and we talk of war tomorrow."

We were soon enjoying the drink, and I spoke enthusiastically about our recent progress in Lundenwic on the farm and our trading activities. Aldren talked of peace throughout Northumbria but how it had led to some disaffection amongst the tribes who saw fighting as their way of life. This occasionally led to conflict in local areas as one group tried to control another. He confirmed his earlier comments that his men were getting older and softer, and they were no longer the force of days gone by. Ecgfrith was a good and fair king and had no great desire to expand his power but would not shirk a battle to protect Northumbria. Soon, the serious talk was over, and we all fell into general banter, typical of men getting drunk.

The bunk beds we had reserved remained unused that night as we fell asleep on the campsite, wrapped in thick blankets provided. If it was cold that night, we didn't notice and woke with thick heads like many around us. Lots of hot, herbal-flavoured drinks helped us to sober up, but looking around, this was not a group of fighting men who you might rely on in battle! It seemed strange to be in comradeship with men of war, but I was learning that it was not always easy for such men to choose their own way of life. We determined to stay amongst the army rather than return to Ripon.

Within a couple of weeks, news began to arrive that the Mercian army was on the move with suggestions of two to three thousand men. Aldren's forces currently amounted to only five hundred men, but tribes were on their way that would take the numbers up to a similar figure as the Mercians. King Ecgfrith had already arrived with a small entourage, but we had not been included in the meetings he held with Aldren and Oldred.

"We'll initially set up to protect the Lindsey and Northumbrian borders with a thousand men," advised Oldred, "and see how the Mercians react. There is no immediate decision on whether we will concede Lindsey, so be ready to fight from the start."

"Are you sure that's what you want?" Tork asked me. "Have you not had any more premonitions?"

"We stay to the end. Nothing has happened to change my mind."

"I notice you don't have any weapons beyond your knives," said Oldred, "I'll ensure you receive shields and spears before the end of the day, and axes, if you want."

As I said nothing, Tork replied, "Let me have all the weapons you mention."

The tension in the camp grew, and the warriors practised their skills. Archers repeatedly sent volleys of arrows across the terrain into straw-filled targets, reminding us that the reality of war was near at hand. Whilst some Mercian scouts were out each day, we used Sher, but the message was the same: the enemy were only two days from the borders.

Dreaming that night of possibly going into battle, my visions were disturbed by that unwelcome voice.

"So, you have heeded my advice and will go to war."

"I gave my word, but can I trust you?"

"Well, if you survive the battle, you will find out about your parents."

"That's not enough. First, are they alive?"

"I'll concede that. They live on, and both are well."

"I need to know how to find them before I will risk killing other people or getting Tork or myself killed."

"We share the same mind, so we both already know, but it is blocked to you until the day you are lined up with Ecgfrith and his overlords ready to fight. So, you will go into battle with the knowledge of where your parents can be found, but you'll have to use your powers to survive the day."

I awoke, this time, less troubled than before, but clear that there was no turning back. Now I just wanted to get things done though I was worried about the outcomes of the battle ahead.

Late the following afternoon, Ecgfrith and his elite warriors were strategically placed to protect their borders when the enemy appeared on the opposite ridge of the valley. Tork and I were alongside Aldren, Oldred and the king, with his men spread out in a defiant manner. I edged forward alongside the king, and he seemed to acknowledge my presence with a slight nod.

"You are Audric, the one who helped our cause at Eoforwic. Aldren told me you have agreed to ride into battle with us."

"Have you decided if we go into battle today?"

"We are in battle already; the Mercians look to take our kingdom."

Looking over the valley, the enemy began to edge forward in a threatening way, raising their shields and banging them with their spears. The noise sent shivers down my spine, and I couldn't wait for the king's decision. I caught his attention and stared intently into his eyes before slowly riding back to Tork.

"Do we ride into battle today?" queried Tork.

"I'm hoping Ecgfrith is about to make that decision."

Suddenly the king raised his spear and pointed back the way. Aldren roared a command reinforcing the message, and we slowly retreated, matching the pace of the enemy advance. This continued for some while until we had reached the border into Northumbria and left Lindsey behind. At this point, we stopped our retreat and were reinforced by the full might of the Northumbrian army spread out over the hillside, looking down on the Mercian warriors who pulled to a halt. The noise had abated, and there was a silence that raised the tension even more than the beating of shields.

If the Mercians recommenced their advance, there would be no stopping the fighting and the resultant bloodbath. The message seemed clear enough - Ecgfrith's men would not retreat further, but did AEthelred understand that Lindsey was being permanently offered to them in return for peace? As those thoughts went through my mind, a further thought took their place. A vision of my parents appeared looking older, but well, working on a farmstead. This vision was suddenly replaced by a sharp image of Angus, the building foreman for the church work in Ripon. Before I could attempt to understand the premonition, a small group of Mercian warriors rode forward.

Tork sat upright and looked in the distance. "This could be it."

My gut tightened as I thought I might still not find my parents if we were to die in battle. "Stay close, Tork; we must see out this day."

As the men around us readied their horses and the silence was lost, Aldren raised his arm, "Hold tight; they have raised a white flag."

Murmuring rose amongst the men, and then Oldred put a similar flag in the air. Ecgfrith moved forward with a small group of warriors. Both enemy groups moved slowly towards each other and then sent individual riders ahead. They talked briefly and then returned. The kings rode forward surrounded by their men, and exchanges lasted until early evening as the sun began to go down.

"So, what do you reckon?" asked Tork.

"It could be a peace settlement if they agree to terms, but I can't be sure."

"Did you know Ecgfrith would concede ground?"

"Not initially, so I couldn't leave it to chance."

"You used your powers on Ecgfrith?"

"Quite so, but unfortunately, I am not close enough to intercede with their current discussions, and we may yet go to war."

The peacemakers united again with their armies, and we edged forward to listen to the conversation.

"There is no war for the moment," shouted Aldren. "We have offered to return the Kingdom of Lindsey to the Mercians, and we will both retreat immediately. Though we did not know it, Lindsey was always their main objective."

There was lots of talking amongst the men, and it was not clear if they were content or disappointed not to be going into battle.

"I'm thankful it worked out, but it was a close thing," I said, looking at a relieved Tork.

"Will you still learn about the existence of your parents?"

"With the battle lines drawn, I had a momentary vision. I think my parents are alive and well and could possibly be in the region."

"But if we had gone into battle, you might never have had the chance to see them."

Oldred rode alongside. "Well, are you happy, my dear friends?"

"Couldn't be happier," said Tork

I smiled and nodded my agreement.

"We'll retreat, leaving a hundred men to watch the border, but we'll stay near Ripon before dispersing," confirmed Oldred.

"We'll do the same but will return to the town tomorrow," I announced.

As we settled back at the original camp near Ripon, the mood amongst the men was one of relief. There were only a few murmurings of discontent, but that was probably more bravado than a real desire for war.

Before sleep took hold, I thought about finding my parents and mentioned to Tork the vivid image of Angus that came in my vision. We speculated but knew that the matter would have to wait until we could find him. I drifted off, trying to hold on to the image of my parents, but a voice soon interrupted my thoughts.

"That was a clever move you pulled hypnotising Ecgfrith."

"Maybe, but he was probably going to concede Lindsey anyway."

"You were lucky the Mercian army didn't just carry straight on through into Northumbria. Would you have stayed to fight?"

"We were committed."

"I don't think we have any more to say to each other. You have your ideology that will never change."

"My hope is that I'll never hear from you again."

"Your journey could have been so much more rewarding."

"If I find my parents, I will never have been happier."

The following morning on the short journey back into Ripon, the air was cool, and the wind was blowing the autumn leaves off the trees. Within weeks, the surrounding forests would lose their beauty, and the stark remains would signal the coming of winter. We headed straight to the church, hoping to find Angus at work, but at first sight, he was not around. Enquiries with the workers suggested he was not far away and had already been down to check progress.

We decided to stay near the building in the hope he would pass by, but before we had time to settle, a booming voice echoed, "You're not resting on the job already; you've just arrived!"

We turned to see Angus looking weather-worn and as rugged as ever.

"You look as though you have managed without us quite well," I retorted. "It's good to see you, and the work on the church is wonderful."

"Thank you. What brings you back this way? We could still use your skills if you want to work," replied Angus.

"It may sound unbelievable, but we've almost been at war against the Mercian army."

"It's no surprise; we've seen a few families heading north saying we could be under attack soon and several tribes heading south to intercept the enemy. So what's happening now?"

"For the moment, there will be peace. Both sides have retreated, and the Northumbrian tribes camped out to the west."

"What's stopped the Mercians advancing?"

"Ecgfrith has conceded Lindsey, and the Mercians seem happy with that."

"Thank God for that, but how did you get involved?"

"That's a bit complicated, but there's a bigger reason why we want to speak with you. Have you ever met a couple called Agra and Stella?"

"Yes, Agra works for me in the forestry area; he started a few months ago. Stella, I've only seen once when they first arrived."

I tried to speak, but the words would not come out.

"They are Audric's parents," explained Tork. "He has not seen them since he was eleven years old."

Angus was astounded. "We've not talked much, perhaps because we have been working so hard, but he never mentioned a son. How did you know to come here to find them?"

"That's part of the complicated story," I offered. "Can I explain later? Is it possible to see my parents now?"

A short while later, we strode through a dense forestry area. I could hear the noise of a tree crashing to the ground, and then, in the distance, I saw three men about to trim the branches.

I quickened my pace and stopped near the men looking intently at the broad shoulders of my father. "Is that you, Father?"

The man dropped his axe, spun around and stared in amazement. "Audric, my boy, but you are a young man now - I barely recognise you."

We moved slowly towards each other and hugged as if our lives depended on it.

"I searched for you everywhere," I said. "Where's Mother?"

"She's fine, strong as an ox and as beautiful as ever. I can't believe we have found each other after all this time. Your mother and I have had quite an ordeal. You look so big. How did you know to find me here?

"Recently, I had this feeling that I should return to Ripon as you both came back into my dreams more and more."

Angus came close, "Leave your work, for now, Agra. Take your son to see his mother."

"Father, this is Tork, a great friend of mine. We've had a few adventures in recent years."

"Your son is a wonderful young man," Tork said. "He has already made his mark in the world and will continue to do so, but above all, he has missed you and his mother."

"Where is Mother? Let's go; we have so much to talk about."

We followed Agra back out of the wood and walked a short distance to a small farm settlement. Out in the fields was a woman tending a flock of sheep.

"There's your mother," said Agra. "Say nothing: see if she recognises you."

Father and I walked ahead, and I sensed our similarity. From a distance, a woman waved as she saw her husband. Then we approached closer, and the woman started to look more intently. By the time we could see each other clearly, she was running towards us and then pulled up a few paces away.

She already knew but said, "Is that you, Audric?" hoping that her mind was not playing tricks. Tears were by now rolling down both our cheeks.

There was an enormous outpouring of emotion that description cannot do justice, but I will never forget.

Back at their dwelling, we sat, reflecting on what had happened to each other over the years. In the raid that sent the families scattering, Mother and Father were taken as prisoners along with several others on the settlement.

My father went on to explain, "At the time, we did not understand why we were chained and roped together over many days whilst more raids took place and further prisoners were taken."

"I always hoped you were alive," I said, "but no one seemed to know what had happened to those not slain in the raid."

"Eventually, we were taken to a shoreline where several longboats were waiting. Everyone boarded, and we set sail. We were at sea for two or three days and held in cramped and sickly conditions before landing in some unknown country."

"By then, we were walking from farm to farm," I explained, "searching for you and others."

Agra continued, "We were separated into pairs and taken by different groups of raiders to inland farm settlements. Fortunately, your mother and I managed to stay together but were put to work on the farmland against our will. Constant threats and occasional physical restraints prevented us from escaping, and we were held in this way for over two years until a few of us made a break one day."

"Slaves by gods," exclaimed Tork. "I wish I could lay my hands on those heathens."

"By then, we had learnt more about the countryside and where we might go, so we headed back to the coastline where we thought we had been brought in by boat. We were not sure who we could trust, so we spent a couple of days wandering around. Eventually, we heard voices in a language we understood, and I took a risk in speaking to them. They were traders who moved goods between the Netherlands and Britain. I wasn't sure what I should tell them, but, in the end, I decided to tell them the full story. Fortunately, they were very sympathetic and agreed to take us back to the northern part of Northumbria, near Alnwick."

"Alnwick," I interrupted, "we must have been so close at times."

"On our return, we sought work at various places to survive, as we have always done, eventually arriving at the former settlement where the raid occurred. However, there was no one there who knew what might have happened to you."

"The family who looked after me returned to the same place each of the next three years to search for you, but we had to keep moving to gain work and a place to live," I explained.

"Like you, we had to travel so we could find work and somewhere to stay, and our search for you never ended. As the years went by, we looked to settle, and a landowner gave us a plot of land to farm. That went well until recently, and so we decided to try our luck in Ripon. We quickly found a new farm to manage, and I got extra work on the church construction. It's still remarkable that you returned to Ripon shortly after our move here. It must be fate."

I was a little stunned, "I can't believe we spent years trying to find each other in Northumbria going round in circles even after you managed to get back to Britain. If that was fate, then it was somewhat cruel."

My mother, Stella, had listened quietly, "Don't worry yourself. It's enough to know you are safe, and we have finally found each other. Whatever has made you into such a fine young man, you must continue with, but please don't leave it so long before coming to see us again."

A smile crossed her face, and we laughed gently.

I filled in the story of my later years but only touched lightly on the link to Morgan and played down some of the more eventful escapades. They were excited by our trading activities

and that we owned the farm in Lundenwic, which they hoped
to see one day.

The evening went on with many new stories until Mother
called a halt. "I'm worn out, and your father needs to rest. He will
need to be back at work early tomorrow. I'm afraid we have no
extra bunks, but you can sleep on the floor."

"Don't worry, we have rooms at the worker's bunkhouse,"
I said. "We'll call back tomorrow when we see the work on the
church closing down for the day. I'm also exhausted; it's been a
very emotional time."

We all stood up, and I hugged my parents again before we
walked out into the evening gloom.

"How are you feeling?" Tork asked.

"It's all been a big shock," I answered, "even though it's what
I've wanted all these years. I couldn't be happier, but the emotion
has worn me out."

"That should settle down soon, and then you can catch up on
some of the life you've missed."

"Thankfully, they survived their ordeal in captivity and look
really well."

"Aye, I can see where you get your strength of character from;
they seem very resilient."

"It poses a bit of a dilemma. Will they want to come back to
Lundenwic, or should I stay here?"

"Don't worry about that for now. Time will offer up a solution.
Enjoy the moment."

In the days ahead, we agreed with Angus to work alongside
my father, and he allowed us to take time off when we wanted it.
Working together, it felt like we had never been apart, chatting
playfully and enjoying the heavy labour. When we returned to
their dwelling, Mother seemed to have a permanent smile on her

face as she watched us together. I occasionally looked across at her and smiled back.

Over the following weeks, we talked about the future, and it was decided that my parents would stay in Ripon until the year-end to help clear all the timbers required for the roof construction. We agreed to stay another week or so and then go back to Lundenwic; then, they would join us later. On our return, we planned to build another dwelling on the farm, which was now busy enough to support more people, especially if Tork and I pursued our ambitions to travel overseas. My parents had listened intently to our plans and felt we should continue to follow our dreams.

Finding my parents was the end of a long journey that had changed my life from a lonely, uncertain boy to a mature, ambitious young man ready to start a new adventure in a world of anticipation and excitement. In reality, our journey had only just begun!

@@@@@@@@@@@@@@

AUDRIC'S WAY

By the lockdown author with nothing better to do, Ken Souyave

Printed in Great Britain
by Amazon

81031295R00109